THE GILDED TREASON

An Alex Hunt Adventure Thriller

URCELIA TEIXEIRA

Independently Published
by
Urcelia Teixeira

Gone too soon!

In loving memory of my father who awakened my sense of adventure by introducing me to Indiana Jones!

Our regular camping trips were spent fishing and diving for lobster & abalone or hiking through Cape Cobra infested mountain paths in Cape Town, South Africa!

Dad, our adventures live on!

Receive a FREE copy of the prequel and see where it all started!

NOT AVAILABLE ANYWHERE ELSE!

Click on image or enter http://download.urcelia.com in your browser

CHAPTER ONE

Southeast Cambodia

Sam's feet wedged beneath the two enormous boulders that lay perched on the edge of the cliff in front of him. He heaved back into the rope he had tied around his waist and then looped around the nearby tree. Sam pulled back hard. He repositioned his one foot as the uneven terrain threatened to throw him off balance. The squeaky sound coming from the rope rubbing against the rugged trunk had him worried. Beads of sweat trickled down his face. The Cambodian jungle was hot and humid, but the sweat on his face was evidence of something far more concerning.

He glanced at the rope chafing against the tree and watched as a single strand unraveled. Beneath his chest his heart thumped hard. He gripped the rope tighter around his hands preparing for the worst and groaned as the scruffy threads of the strained rope sliced into the flesh of his bare hands.

Five-hundred feet below the sheer cliff edge, at the other end of the rope, Alex searched the rock wall behind the cascade of water falling from above her head. Rappelling had never appealed to her, but she could hardly hold Sam's weight over the steep thousand feet waterfall, so the duty lay on her to descend the steep cliff. The icy cold spray from the water had her drenched, and her feet slipped against the smooth, wet surface of the cliff side. Masses of water poured down from the waterfall's edge above her head. What was she thinking? She hated heights, she doubted, reasoning that perhaps she shouldn't have looked down into the frothy white water that smashed into the rocks below. Alex shut her eyes tight as she battled to control her breathing, frustrated over the fact that she thought her agoraphobia was under control, especially considering everything she had been through chasing after Rhapta. Recalling how far she'd come she finally opened her eyes again and looked straight ahead into the side of the cliff.

Conscious of her harness cutting into her groin as it carried her entire weight, she allowed her hands to glide against the stone wall in search of an opening. The century-old map handed to them by the police commissioner showed there was supposed to be ancient tunnels to a hidden temple in the rock face behind the waterfall.

"There's nothing, Sam! Just solid rock surface and water!"

Lots, the thought echoed in her head.

Then, without warning, she suddenly plunged several feet before coming to a dead halt, bashing her shoulder hard against the wall.

"SAM!" she screamed upwards toward the top of the cliff.

Out of her eyesight Sam found himself lying face down in the dirt, his hands gripping the rope for dear life. His cheek was on fire where the cord had slapped him across his face when the last strand broke free from the tree behind him. Somehow, he had managed to catch the end of the rope just before it had a chance to disappear over the cliff and consequently plunging Alex into a watery death. It now took every bit of his physical and mental strength to hold on.

"Sam! Pull me up!" Alex shouted while she frantically searched the entirely smooth wall with her hands for something to grab onto. Strands of wet hair lay across her face, making it nearly impossible to see anything. Why wasn't he answering? she thought.

"S-A-M! What's happening up there? Pull me up!"

"I - I'm try-ing." He forced out a soft, barely audible shout under the immense strain of her pendulous weight.

Sam eventually released enough tension in the rope to allow his wrist around it twice and managed to do the same with his other hand. Having been in a standing position just about took all he had, but lying face down had him in an awkward position of having to rely on the strength of his arms alone, even with a firmer grip.

Alex faced certain death. He shut his eyes and tugged hard at the rope using its leverage to get on his knees and slowly back onto his feet. Once up, he twisted his body around the rope and once again found his footing against the boulders.

"Alex! You okay?" finally able to speak loud enough for her to hear.

"Sure! I'm admiring the view while you take your time pulling me up!" she said annoyed. She was oblivious to the dire circumstances that unraveled on the cliff's edge high above her dangling body.

Sam ignored her sarcastic stab and remained focussed on the straining rope cutting into his flesh.

"Do you have any footing?" he asked.

"No, nothing!"

It wasn't the answer he had hoped to hear. Sam's eyes remained pinned on the three untangled strands of cord now eroding against the sharp edge of the cliff in front of him. He instantly regretted giving in to her. Not that he would have convinced her otherwise. Alex was relentless in pursuing a challenge, no matter the cost.

"You're going to have to keep the rope steady on your side, okay? Try not to move too much and find something to grab onto!" Sam shouted.

His feet pushed down firmly on the ground as he heaved, prayer the rope would hold up. Another cord snapped, and he found himself wondering how many strings the rope had. Eight? Twelve? He pushed the threatening negative thoughts from his mind and continued gently working at pulling her up. What felt like an eternity, his eyes eventually caught sight of Alex's hands as the tip of her fingers appeared over the edge of the rocky cliff.

The victory had been short-lived when another cord suddenly snapped just as he spotted the top of her head above the cliff's edge. He swore under his strained breathing.

"Climb, Alex! I'm not sure the rope is going to hold!" he heaved.

As reality suddenly dawned on her, the anguished look in her eyes was enough to have Sam risk it all and give one final hard pull. The remaining threads in the rope instantly snapped and deposited Sam flat on his back in the dirt.

"Alex!" he scrambled to the cliff's edge where Alex clung for dear life off the side of the rock face.

"Help me, Sam! I can't hold on any longer."

She was barely within Sam's reach but managed to grab hold of a thin vine root about three feet down the side of the cliff. Closing her hand tighter onto the root that wasn't long enough for her other hand to grab onto much less strong enough to hold her full weight, Alex fought to gain control of the situation.

"Look at me, Alex! I've got you. Give me your hand."

"I can't."

"Yes, you can!"

Sam wasn't all too sure he would ever forget the look of desperation in Alex's eyes that had already pooled with tears.

"Alex, you're going to have to give me your free hand. I'll catch you, I promise."

"I don't know if I can. Please don't let me fall," she started a faint sob, her eyes pinned on his outstretched hand.

"Alex, look at me. I'm not going to let you fall. We have a relic to find, and an entire country is depending on you. You're going to grab my hand when I count it down, and I'm going to pull you up, okay? You can do this. I'm not letting you die here today, you hear me?"

She barely nodded, her teary eyes remaining locked with his. Sam had curled his one foot around a watermelon-sized rock in the hope that it would sustain both their weights. He stretched both hands out toward Alex's hand as far as his body would allow it. His fingertips just about touched her knuckles where she still gripped the root. There simply wasn't any room for error, Sam reminded himself, concealing the fear and doubt in his eyes as he started the countdown.

"Three...two...one!"

Alex let go of the root and propelled her lean body upward as she stretched both her hands toward Sam's. Her one hand firmly latched onto his but, failing to swing her body high enough for the other hand to fully grab hold of his, yielded Sam's fingertips barely hooking underneath her own. Sam groaned under the strain of his outstretched body. It felt as if all the tendons in his arm were ripping from his shoulder bones.

"Sam, my fingers are slipping." Her hands were still wet from the water spray. "I can't hold on."

"I've got you, Alex." Sam's words strained as he clung to her one hand with all he had. "You're not dying here today, do you hear me? I'm going to hoist you up enough for you to grab onto my other arm, okay? I've got you."

He wasn't sure he had the strength to even pull her up another inch and he needed convincing himself as his arm burned under the immense strain. But he dared not show it. He bit down hard onto his teeth and somehow managed to lift her just enough so she could grab tightly onto his wrist. His foot stretched around the sharp rock cutting into his ankle. The stone was the only leverage he had. It had to hold up. Careful to not slide over the cliff, he drew back until he could sit up on his knees and pull her up by the waist of her pants. Paralyzed with fear, Alex threw her arms around his neck and clung to him like a small child would a parent on the first day of school.

Over the last couple of years they had grown quite close. There had been times it veered on perhaps too close in a working relationship, but right here, right now, they couldn't care. She needed him as much as he needed her.

"Well, that didn't quite go down the way we planned," he finally said in an attempt to relieve the awkwardness of their embrace. Alex's tender weeping instantly became a subdued giggle in response. She pulled back and wiped her face with her t-shirt.

Walking to retrieve her backpack from under the tree, she found herself questioning if this was what she had signed up for. Since her father's retirement, she had been on several expeditions in the role of head archaeologist at the uni, but nothing quite as death defeating as this.

"Tell me how we ended up in the middle of the Cambodian jungle again, please?" Sam dryly added as he got up and untied the broken rope that still dangled from his waist.

"We're hired hands, Sam Quinn. I guess this is just another day in the lives of the world's two top archaeologists," she said in jest as she wiped the tears from her cheek and swept her hair back.

"Ah yes, hired hands. You never actually told me how much they're paying us though. It had better be worth risking our lives for."

"It will do just fine Sam. Not that it matters much at this stage. Thus far none of the clues are adding up, so there's no payment until we prove the authenticity of the stolen golden urn. So if you're done lying around, I suggest we head back and go over our intel again."

Sam watched her put on a brave show but her pale face and trembling hands were a dead giveaway.

"You're still shaking, Alex. Let's just rest for a moment," rubbing his sore shoulder.

"It's as good as it's going to get, Sam. No point agonizing over it."

Sam beamed with pride at her show-must-go-on answer. He had always appreciated her courage and determination. Alex Hunt was a woman who could pretty much get out of any sticky situation and tackled any challenge head-on. Unlike any of the other woman he had ever known. She possessed an inner strength coupled with immense courage. After Tanzania, she had become a changed person. A woman who would stop at nothing until the quest was complete.

Sam dusted off his hat and placed it back on his head only to see Alex had already disappeared into the shoulder high thorny shrubs behind him.

T he equatorial sun beat down hard through the dense forest canopy. Alex glanced periodically at her satellite driven navigation device as they pushed through the thorn-studded shrubs back to their vehicle. The hour-long trek to the Toyota Cruiser felt like an eternity. Neither spoke while they digested the near fatal incident back at the waterfall. It was hot, and maneuvering through the thick leaves took immense effort.

"We had better hurry Quinn. The sun is sitting low already, and I don't know about you, but I'd hate to spend the night here."

"Right behind you Alex. These pestering red ants have a nasty bite," whacking one that managed to get to his ankle under his pants.

The Cambodian jungle wasn't a comfortable place to be in at all. The thorny shrubs ripped their arms and faces and navigating through the ankle high vines across the forest floor was exhausting.

"We should be close. Tomorrow we head back to the Commissioner-General's office. There has to be something we missed."

"I don't see how we missed anything, Alex. We went through the map and all the details of the police report with a fine-toothed comb. Unless of course..." Sam paused.

"Unless what?"

"Unless they purposefully left something off the report."

"Why would they do that? They hired us to unearth the legend of an original urn in the first place. That's why they flew us out here. That theory doesn't make any sense, Sam."

"Indeed, but what if the Buddhist followers are right and the stolen urn really is a fake? The government would try to cover it up, right? I mean, can you imagine the persecution if the people found out that the holy urn they've been worshipping all this time had been a fake? It would start a civil war!"

"Well, what if it wasn't a fake? What if it was the real relic and you're barking up the wrong tree here, Sam?"

Sam whacked another mosquito on the back of his neck.

"Hmm, might be but I recall reading the police report wondering how the perpetrators got past the guards outside the shrine in the first place. I might not be a detective, but I certainly picked up some discrepancies in that report."

Alex stopped and checked the coordinates she wrote in her notebook.

"What's wrong?" Sam asked

"We should be right on the spot where we left the Cruiser. I don't understand."

"You sure?"

"Hundred percent, look. Here are the tracks, and the leaves are flattened where it was parked. There's the road."

Sam walked over to the clearing where they had parked the Cruiser earlier that morning. She was right. It was the right spot. The vehicle showed tracks coming in, fresh oil stains on the leaves where it stood and then new tracks up ahead.

"Tell me it's not what I'm thinking."

"I wish I could but it certainly looks like we were the victims of vehicle theft, Miss Hunt," Sam commented with a snicker.

"You find this funny Sam? We're at least six hours on foot from the nearest village, and in case you haven't noticed, it will be dark soon."

"Oh, I noticed. But I can hardly cry now, can I? Perhaps you and I should cozy up in a hollow somewhere. Reminds me of our first exploration in Tanzania, come to think of it."

"Hardly," throwing herself down on the flattened parking spot to drink water and study the roadmap.

"This jungle is full of dangerous animals, and they are far more densely populated than those in the African bush. Come on. We follow the tracks and hopefully we can catch up to whoever stole our vehicle. Something tells me we have some evildoers trying to sabotage our efforts. My gut tells me there's more to finding this urn than what meets the eye."

As quickly as she sat down, she got up again and walked off following the Cruiser's tracks.

"Can I have a drink of water first, please? I know you dangled in the crisp waters of the waterfall, but I, on the other hand, haven't quite recovered from that almost fatal ordeal."

"Well, since you saved me, I can barely refuse," clicking away on her Sat Nav.

"Hmm, that's strange," she let out after a couple of minutes of silence.

"What?"

"The Sat Nav brought us here, but it's not picking up any roads ahead. Both the tracks and the road run dead here."

She switched the gadget off then on again and rechecked the map.

"Surely they would have had to drive off somewhere. It's bizarre," Alex commented feeling puzzled.

"We don't have much time until it's dark Alex. We need to get a move on. With any luck we'll pick up fresh tracks."

＊

Night fell and, after hours in the treacherous jungle, there was still no sign of their vehicle, its tracks or any roads.

"That's impossible," Alex exclaims. "How could they have just disappeared into thin air?"

Sam giggled, as was now typical in his effort to diffuse her obvious annoyance with the situation.

"They didn't Alex. The vegetation changed, so the tires didn't leave any marks, that's all."

Alex looked around at the vines and small twigs that covered the ground. She contemplated if perhaps a professional tracker would have been able to trace them, but to her untrained eye it was nearly impossible to detect which direction the thieves had gone into.

"Yes well, now what? This doesn't help us much, does it? We're lost. I haven't the foggiest where in this jungle we are."

"You're tired. Let's take a break and try to make a camp for the night. It's going to be dark soon and we won't be able to see anything anyway."

Sam knew her edginess was nothing personal. It was clear the waterfall incident came too close for comfort and that she needed to digest it properly. His years in the medical field taught him to look beyond what people's exterior revealed.

Sam scratched the back of his head as he plotted how to build a shelter of some sorts while Alex continued pacing around the same tree.

"So I guess we're in a bit of a fix here. The jungle is fraught with anything from venomous constrictors and panthers to tigers and even bears. We can't be on the ground, and we can't be in the trees either. Oh, and let's not forget the wild elephants," she said annoyed.

Sam started unpacking his backpack, ignoring her rant before calmly sayin, "Fire. We need a fire. Think you can put one together while I get a shelter going?"

It was the distraction she needed and within minutes Alex had a fire going while Sam's apt survival skills slowly produced a floor of bamboo poles tied together with the leftover rope from the waterfall fiasco. Another three poles stood in a tripod shape over the spread floor, which he had covered with large leaves. He stood back, hands on his hips and admired his creation.

"That should do it. Not too shabby for a first timer in the jungle if I can say so myself. The machete certainly did the trick."

"You're right, not too bad at all. Perhaps the jungle brings out a bit of Tarzan in you," she scoffed, now in a slightly better state of mind.

"Yes well, ahem, Jane, what's for dinner?"

"Shh! What's that?" Alex froze stiff at a huffing sound coming from behind Sam.

"What? I don't hear anything," Sam whispered back.

"Shhh!"

Moments later a fully grown black bear appeared out of nowhere and just about knocked Alex's breath from her lungs.

"Don't move Sam," she managed to say in a subdued voice.

"Don't move? Why? Tell me it's not a giant tarantula on my back. I hate spiders."

"Okay, it's not a tarantula, but it is infact a bear, and a large one at that. Just don't run. Move toward me. Slowly! Whatever you do, DON'T RUN," she added slowly with emphasis.

Alex's eyes remained fixed on the bear who was about twenty feet behind Sam. Sam moved slowly toward Alex until he passed her and then cautiously turned around and faced the bear. Saliva dripped between his clenched jaw, his upper lip pulled upward to reveal his sharp teeth as he growled. It was obvious the animal was out in search of dinner.

"Now what?" Sam whispered nervously with his hands in the air as if he was held at gunpoint.

"Well, start by lowering your arms. He's not holding a gun as far as I can see."

"Right okay, of course."

Sam lowering his arms somehow agitated the bear even further, and without warning, it stood up on its hind legs and towered over them with a loud hissing sound warning them that he meant business.

"Uhh, that's not a good sign Alex."

The surprise visit had them completely unprepared.

"We should shout and make ourselves look big," Sam suggested.

"Aren't we supposed to roll into a ball? I'm sure I read this somewhere," Alex responded.

"I'll shout, and you roll into a ball, best of both worlds. What do you think?"

"I think you're stone crazy, Sam Quinn, but let's give it a try. Don't see any other way out."

Like an arrow from a bow, Alex dropped to the ground and rolled herself into a fetal position while Sam shouted and flapped his arms above his head. The bear growled and hissed back. His massive paws stretched upward while he walked on his hind legs, moving closer and closer to his prey.

"I don't think this is working, Alex! We should make a run for it."

Sam had barely spoken his words when a single gunshot resounded through the air and they watched as the bear thud to the ground and landed flat on his back, paws outstretched.

"What the...?" Sam exclaimed hands in the air again.

"Crikey Mate. Did you think those moves of yours would scare him away? By the looks of it, the only one to run would be your Sheila here."

The stranger's voice flung both Alex and Sam around in one quick motion. Behind Sam stood the likes of someone who looked like he had been raised in the jungle. Tall and tanned from head to toe, dressed in khaki shorts and a broad-rimmed black hat decorated with animal fur and fangs. In his hands, he held the still smoking rifle he had just used to shoot the bear between the eyes.

"G'day Mate, Sheila," tipping his hat at Alex.

"She'll be right, no worries."

Alex, who didn't understand a word he said, glanced questioningly at Sam and the dumbstruck pair watched in silence as the odd man walked over to his kill, lifting the gigantic paws and dropping it to the ground.

"It's a real shame, ain't it, Mate? Such a beauty. You had Buckley's chance against it though. Ten more seconds and he'd have ripped you apart. They don't eat humans but you must have disturbed his nocturnal hunt or something. Will make a ripper stew tonight nonetheless. The name's Ollie, Mate, short for Oliver," wiping his hands on his pants as he walked over to Sam inviting a handshake.

"Quinn, Dr Sam Quinn and this is Alexandra Hunt."

"Alex, actually. Only my parents call me by my full name," Alex spoke.

"Well, pleased to meet your acquaintance. Now, unless you want to face another Asian bear or a panther, we best be moving on."

Alex and Sam watched as the stranger untied the tripod structure and started fastening the bear's paws to the pole.

Sam whispered to Alex as they stood back and allowed their rescuer to finish off. "Okay, don't get me wrong. I'm elated this bloke saved us from sure death, but he's weird."

"I think he's Australian," Alex whispered back.

"Good on ya, Alexandra. G'd ol' Down Under. Now stop your pissing about, Mate and help me carry our dinner."

"Dinner! Oh no, I don't eat bear meat. I'm quite fine, thank you very much. And it's Alex, not Alexandra."

"Yeah well, *Alex*, when you've lived here for as long as I have you make use of what the earth provides. And this old bear didn't kick the bucket for nothing."

The Aussie's beady brown eyes were friendly and in perfect harmony to his upbeat, energetic personality.

"Well, I won't say no. I'm famished," Sam chimed in and started pulling alongside Ollie as they made their way through the lush green jungle.

CHAPTER TWO

I t was another two-hour walk before they reached a narrow pathway that led to a medium-sized wooden house on stilts. Sam found it hard to hide his surprise and admiration. "Is this your house? It's incredible! I've never seen anything like it."

Alex, on the other hand, tried her best not to drop her guard and show her wonderment. "It's quite something all right."

The two men stopped and put the dead animal down in a small clearing next to the house. Sam, still in a state of astonishment, walked back to the front of the house to join Alex. Ollie didn't answer. Instead, he searched the perimeter of the house and walked up the stairs onto the wraparound porch.

"Sam, look there," Alex whispered beckoning toward the several surveillance cameras hidden in the trees around the house.

"All right, you two, the coast is clear."

Clear from what? Alex thought but followed Sam up the stairs onto the deck and into the house where Ollie shoved a beer into each of their hands.

"Cheers Mate," he said, as he whacked his beer against theirs and downed half the bottle.

"Ah, nothing like an ice-cold stubby to quench the thirst, hey?" downing the other half before reaching inside his refrigerator for another one.

The ice-cold beer in Alex's hand was too tempting. So much so that even her stubborn pride couldn't prevent her from taking several mouthfuls, ignoring Ollie's sheepish grin in response.

"So what brings you two Brits out here in the middle of nowhere? The jungle isn't a place to go walkabout, you know? You can count your lucky stars I bumped into you. That bamboo tent of yours wouldn't have kept the fastest rat safe from the tigers and snakes."

A very enthusiastic Sam took another gulp of his beer before replying, "We really appreciate it, Ollie, thanks. Not sure what we would have done if you hadn't shown up. We were out at the waterfall and our Cruiser seemed to have vanished into thin air."

Ollie cracked open his second beer and handed another to Sam.

"Now that's a bugger, Mate. You sure you went back to where you left it?"

"Oh, I don't make mistakes with coordinates," Alex snapped.

"Just saying, Sheila. For it to disappear like that it would have had to be stolen. Not unlikely, given the fact that this part of the jungle harbors many insurgent groups."

Ollie put his beer down and opened his laptop. Two clicks later he slammed the lid shut and walked back over to Sam.

"So Mate, what do you say we go cut up that dinner of ours before the cats come for it? I'm starving. The missus can freshen up so long."

Alex just about choked on a mouthful of beer. "Missus! Oh no, we're not married or anything. Sam is my assistant."

Ollie paused, scanning his eyes over Sam. "Is that right, hey? Assistant, like a secretary or something?"

Instantly regretting her bad choice of words, Alex set off to redeem Sam's honor, "No-no, not like that. We're archaeologists, and I simply head up the team. Sam is my very esteemed colleague, helping me in the field and such."

"Well, what do you know? Where I come from, the Sheilas assist the blokes, not the other way around. But, hey, each kangaroo to its own."

Sam didn't seem to be too bothered by their host's prejudice remark, but Alex could feel her blood curdle beneath her clammy skin, partly by virtue of her own stupidity.

Ollie downed the last of his beer before adding, "Well, then you'll be flipping a coin for the bed tonight. The loser will have to take the couch." He turned his eyes to Alex. "The dunny is outside, and there's a shower cubicle next to it. Spare towels are in the cupboard over there. There shouldn't be any wild animals pestering you. They can't come close without tripping the snares, but you best be taking that lamp with you just to be safe. We'll keep an eye out for you."

Wild animals, snares, outside shower! Are you kidding me? Alex thought, clearly agonized by the mere notion of showering in the pitch black darkness out in the middle of a jungle. But she was sticky from the hike and desperate for a shower, so she turned and headed toward the cupboard for a towel none-theless, grateful to have a reason to leave their brash host. She watched them turn and head off to the bottom of the stairs.

"Wait! What's a dunny?" she shouted at Ollie.

Ollie belted a laugh loud enough that it echoed through the trees and continued walking down the stairs ignoring her. When Sam turned to go back up the stairs to explain, Ollie grabbed his arm, "No worries, Mate. She'll figure it out," sporting another wave of laughter.

A lex soon found the 'dunny' to mean a toilet, which was nothing, but a deep hole in the ground with a neatly cut out hole in a camp chair positioned over it. It very nearly turned her stomach upside down and forced her to cover her nose with her t-shirt in a futile attempt to escape a stench so foul it alone was enough to keep any jungle creature away. But even that thought wasn't enough to convince her of being safe from any prowling animals. The front of the jungle bathroom was completely open and exposed, and the only privacy it provided was a cordoned off bamboo fence covering it on each of its three sides.

A toilet roll hung from a wire protruding from the bamboo fence, and a curled up car magazine sat wedged between two poles in front of it. To the right was a bucket of sand and a spade. Never in all the years of traveling with her parents had she ever seen anything like this. She concluded that she'd much rather duck behind a shrub than risk that contraption.

A few feet away her eye caught sight of a similar bamboo cubicle housing a large metal container with a saucepan on top of it.

Alex thought she had seen it all. She lifted the lid off to find it filled with what she had hoped would be fresh water. It wasn't. Instead, a trapped frog jumped out as soon as the lid came off, causing her to drop it noisily back onto the container. Again, the cubicle had been covered only on three sides, while her back was left completely exposed to the pitch-black jungle behind her. The lamp in her hand offered very little light, but it would have to do. She was desperate for a wash, albeit in her birthday suit in the middle of the jungle with a saucepan or three of stale water.

But, much to her surprise the jungle bathing was better than she had expected. Primal to say the least, but there was something so pure and natural about the experience that it had left her somewhat relaxed. Deep in thought, her eye caught the swift blinking of a red light below a surveillance camera that was attached to a tree, the lens aimed directly at the shower. And then it dawned on her.

"Oh, the pervert! Wait till I get my hands around your throat Ollie or Oliver or whoever you say you are!" She exclaimed while throwing her clothes on and stomping up the dark path toward where the two of them were busy gathering their slaughter.

"Just what exactly do you think you're doing? How dare you?"

A surprised Sam flung around mere seconds before an equally surprised Ollie followed suit.

"It's just a bear Sheila, relax. You'll probably find you'll enj—"

"I'm not talking about the bear, you pervert!" she cut in. "Is this what you do out here in the jungle, huh? Film naked women who you probably lure here. I wouldn't be surprised if it was you who stole our vehicle. The perfect plan to—"

"Whoa, Sheila, calm down. You're chasing the wrong bone here," Ollie replied in a futile attempt to calm her down.

"Of course you'd say that. Where's the recording?" Alex didn't wait for an answer and stormed off up the stairs to where his laptop stood on the table inside the jungle house. Her mind raced through what seemed very obvious to her, finding it hard to still her pounding heart beneath her anger.

Sam came running up behind her, "Alex, what on earth's the matter with you? It's hardly a polite way to talk to someone taking us in for the night. What's gotten into you?"

"Ha, polite talk, you're joking right? Do you think our host is polite in recording me taking a shower? Polite, my foot!" she shouted as she flipped the laptop's lid open.

"What are you talking about? He was with me the entire time."

"The cameras, Sam! They're all over the place. And he knew there's one facing the shower. That's what he was switching on with his computer earlier. He got it all on tape."

"No, I didn't," Ollie interrupted, exceptionally calm for a man who just got busted. "They're not cameras. They are motion sensors. The red light means it's off. Green is on."

Ollie nonchalantly walked over to the basin, washed his hands and started preparing the meat. On the other side of the tree house, Alex sat staring in silence at Ollie's blank computer screen on her lap. Sam wiped his hands on a cloth, bent down and whispered to her.

"You are imagining things, Alex. For reasons not quite understood by me, I sense you don't like the man, but he's nothing but a decent guy seeking solitude in the jungle. A guy who saved us from being mauled by a bear and who is putting us up for the night when he didn't have to. Not everyone is evil, you know."

Sam kneeled on one knee in front of her and went quiet for a bit before he spoke again. "Perhaps you need to take your meds tonight, Alex."

"No way! I don't need the pills. I haven't taken them since, Rhapta. I'm not overreacting, Sam."

Sam's raised eyebrow in response challenged her last comment.

"Fine. So I was perhaps wrong to assume those were cameras, but why would he need motion sensors in the middle of the jungle in the first place? And pretty sophisticated looking ones at that. I'm telling you. He's hiding something."

She slammed the laptop closed and walked out onto the porch with Sam following a few steps behind her. Her eyes focused on each device nailed to the trees all around the cabin. All the lights were green except for the one above the shower. She bit the inside of her lip as she realized Ollie had told the truth. Noticing it, Sam didn't have to rub it in, so he kept quiet. It was good for her to be suspicious in these circumstances considering what had happened back in Tanzania. It had only been two years after all, and the uni made sure her expedition workload was not too taxing for her to handle. She had been off the pills all this time, so she had more than proven herself capable of coping with the challenges at hand with each new mission. But perhaps the fact that she had almost died at the waterfall earlier that day and the discovery of their stolen Cruiser triggered something inside her. None of the expeditions over the last couple of years were dangerous or threatening in any way; this one, not so much.

"It's been a long day, Alex. Maybe you just need to rest. We'll be safe here tonight. I'll sleep with one eye open."

Alex bit the flesh around her thumbnail while Sam continued his attempt to reassure her.

"We'll head back to the hotel tomorrow, and then we can carry on with our mission to find the golden urn, okay? Just sit outside here for a bit and try to relax."

Alex nodded as she watched Sam grab a towel and head for the shower. She looked back with wariness at Ollie where he was still busy preparing the bear stew in the kitchen. He hadn't uttered a word since her outburst and whilst she owed him an apology, her gut told her she wasn't wrong not to trust him fully. Something didn't quite sit right with this guy. He was all Aussie and happy go lucky, a big ball of cheer, but her instincts had never been wrong. Ollie might fool Sam, but not her.

When they finally sat down for dinner, her suspicions were further piqued when she accidentally dropped her fork under her chair. She bent down to pick it up, and her eye caught sight of a pistol taped to the bottom of the table where Ollie sat. Sam noticed something in her eyes as she shuffled back into her seat but didn't comment.

"Tuck in Sheila. Once you taste bear-meat, you'll never go back to lamb. With any luck his last meal was berries."

"I'm not hungry, thanks, and please, call me Alex." She was starving, in truth, but she wouldn't give him the satisfaction, especially because he kept calling her Sheila.

Sam cleared his throat, hinting for her not to be rude and to eat something, only to get a kick in the shin in return which made him smile.

"So, Ollie, how long have you been living here?" Alex ventured, inviting another glare from Sam.

"Not long enough, Sheila," irritating her on purpose. "I love it out here. As long as I mind my own business and stay out of trouble."

"So you're living here on your own then?" ignoring his obvious temptation to further crawl under her skin. She was far more focused on figuring out who he was and why he didn't give her a straight answer.

"Indeed. How about some rice at least, huh? After a day like today surely you must be hungry? Come on. I promise I didn't poison it."

Alex sensed he was trying to change the topic by evading her questions while clearly attempting to evoke a reaction from her.

"I wouldn't mind some more thanks, Ollie," Sam responded in an attempt to ease the tension around the dinner table. "You're right. This stew is like nothing I've ever tasted."

Alex wasn't going to let up her inquiry by making small talk over the stupid stew.

"Why do you need motion sensors around your house, and why did you say, 'the coast is clear' when we arrived? Clear from who?"

"Are you always so suspicious of everyone, Sheila? In case you haven't noticed. We are in the middle of a jungle with wild animals all around us. I have snares set up all around my house, and the motion sensors act as an alarm if they managed to escape the traps somehow and come too close. Satisfied?"

He didn't wait for her to answer.

"Now, it seems I'm not the only one that should come under interrogation. You never answered my question. What are the two of you doing out here?"

Alex glanced at Sam across the table who tucked into the food like there was no tomorrow.

"Not that it's any of your business, really, but as I said earlier, we are archaeologists out here on an expedition."

"To find what? Archaeologists only come out here if they're onto something. What are you looking to find? Perhaps I can be of some help."

"Oh, I seriously doubt that very much!" Alex sneered as she straightened her fork next to her plate.

"A golden urn," Sam answered in between two more bites, ignoring Alex's angry stare in response.

"Now what do you know? So you're the pair they hired to find it? How lucky can I be? Well then, let me volunteer my services to help you catch the buggers who stole it. I have some skills, and connections, that might be of worth to you, I reckon."

Ollie sat back in his chair and sported an arrogant smirk as he waited for Alex to answer with some snarly remark.

"Do you now? And what skills are those?" she finally caved.

"Well, for starters, I speak Mandarin fluently. I don't suppose you do?"

Alex felt her insides heat up in response to his smug revelation.

"I speak French, and we've been able to get around just fine."

"French might help with the older generation, but if you're relic hunting around here, you'd need to speak either Mandarin or Khmer. You would also have to go underground. The word on the street is that it was an inside job; possibly a black market operation. The urn is worth a small fortune on the black market. If it does contain Buddha's remains as they say, then it could have been taken by anyone. Vietnam, Thailand, China, Japan, heck, even India. They've been fighting over the ownership for centuries."

"That's if it were, in fact, the actual artifact they stole in the first place." It was Alex's turn to look smug.

Her comment had precisely the effect she aimed it would have on Ollie as he immediately sat up and leaned forward.

"What do you mean? You think it was a fake?"

Sam had finally finished his second plate of food and joined the conversation.

"Exactly, there are rumors that the temple had a counterfeit one on display all these years. The monks are up in arms about it.

"Although we don't know that for certain. It is possible, but there's no proof of either at this stage," Alex intervened.

"So the commissioner hired the two of you to hunt down the urn and prove the stolen one's authenticity, interesting." Ollie sat back in his chair again and folded his arms across his chest.

When Sam finally put his cutlery down and rubbed his full tummy with satisfaction he added.

"We have been following several leads over the recent couple of weeks, and each one sent us on a wild goose chase. The last of which led us to believe we'd find the urn in hidden tunnels belonging to a temple that was meant to lie concealed behind the waterfall. But there was no evidence of any temple ruins or tunnels anywhere. Alex almost died out there today when the rope chafed through and broke."

"Crikey, Sheila, no wonder you're peeved at the world. Wait. I've got just the thing for you."

Ollie bolted across the room like a firecracker on New Year's Eve to retrieve a glass jar of clear liquid and a couple of glasses from the kitchen cupboard.

"This should calm those nerves of yours in no time."

Before Alex could object, she had a small tot glass in her hand, and raised into the air.

"Cheers Mates, here's to finding the precious golden urn."

The liquid might have looked like water but it most certainly wasn't, and Alex found herself struggling to breathe much less talk after she swigged it back.

Ollie belted a laugh so loud he just about fell off his chair.

"Well, Sheila. Now I know how to keep you quiet."

If Alex could speak—or move—she'd have punched that grin straight off his face.

"It's a bit strong even for me, Ollie. What is it?" Sam came to her rescue, still trying to get his own breath back.

"My very own home-brewed moonshine. Made from the finest ingredients right in my backyard, Mate. Puts hair on your chest, doesn't it? Here, have another one," filling Sam's glass with another shot.

Sam watched as the alcohol-induced spasm finally wore off enough for Alex to take a deep breath and gulp down a glass of water.

"Ha! Water won't help, Sheila. Eat a chunk of bread."

Alex had no choice but to give in to his suggestion, though it went against every fiber of her stubborn being and unfortunately for her, he was right. It helped, somewhat. Enough for her to get up and gather the plates in a feeble attempt to try gain control of the situation and escape Ollie's mocking gaze.

Sam noticed Alex went from neutral to red to pale green.

"Right then, Ollie. Dinner was delicious, but if you'd show us to your spare bedroom, I think we'd better call it a night," taking the plates from Alex's hands and setting it on the edge of the kitchen sink.

"Down there to the left, Mate. We'll hunt down your Cruiser in the morning. I'll make a couple of calls to my connections and see what I can find out."

"We'd appreciate that, thank you," Sam replied.

"Oh, I don't feel too good," Alex groaned, catching them both by surprise. Seconds later, she bolted for the porch and made it just in time to deposit her paltry stomach contents over the railing.

"Firewater for a firecracker," Ollie teased afterward as he launched a bucket of water over the railing.

Alex felt her cheeks glow underneath part embarrassment and part anger. She fought back the urge to shout a few unladylike words at him, choosing to instead storm off to the bedroom where she slammed the room's door behind her. Battling to maintain her composure, she heard Sam politely thank Ollie for his hospitality and moments later joined her in the room.

"Why are you so angry with the guy, Alex? What has he done to make you dislike him so much?"

"I don't know, Sam, but something isn't right. He's not all he portrays to be. I know it. I want to get out of here, Sam. As soon as the sun comes up, we start walking. Do you hear me? This brute can shove his bear stew right up his friendly Aussie you know what!"

"Easy there tiger. I think you need to sleep it off. We'll figure it all out in the morning, okay?"

Sam knew all too well not to even try talking any sense into Alex when she was convinced of something, but he also knew she was clearly traumatized and needed rest more than anything right now. When she finally fell asleep in the bed, he settled into his make-shift bed of blankets and pillows on the floor beside her.

CHAPTER THREE
Phnom Penh, Cambodia

When morning broke Ollie's 'connections' somehow did come through for them and although their vehicle was still missing, Alex and Sam did manage to catch a ride with his associates—as Ollie had put it—into the city. Alex had no idea who they were nor did she care. All she wanted was to get away from Ollie and back to the safety of her clean hotel room in Phnom Penh.

By the time they had reached their hotel, the foyer was already bustling with guests making their way to the dining area for breakfast. Though the hotel wasn't quite the five stars it claimed to be, it was nonetheless a huge relief to be back. At the very least she'd have fresh running water and a decent shower and toilet.

At the end of the poorly lit corridor leading to their adjoining rooms Alex noticed the door to her room slightly ajar.

"What on earth...?"

"Shh!" Sam hushed her. He pulled a gun from his waistband under his shirt and pushed her against the wall behind him.

"Why do you have a gun with you?" She whispered in surprise.

"Ollie reckoned it might be a good idea; in the event of an eventuality. Stay here."

"Not going to happen. I'm coming with you."

Sam knew not to argue and noticed his room door slightly open too. They walked along the wall of the corridor and stopped just outside Alex's room to listen. It was quiet so he slowly pushed the door open with the tip of the silver Smith & Wesson revolver's barrel. Alex stayed behind him. There was no sign of anyone inside the small room or her bathroom.

Behind them, the door to his room creaked.

"Stay here, Alex!" Sam whispered in a stern voice as he hastened into his room and watched the figure of a man escaping over the balcony.

"Hey! Stop!"

But Sam was too late and he watched as the intruder jumped the two stories and escaped across the street.

"Sam!" Alex shouted in a panicked voice from her room. Sam sprinted back to her room expecting to find an accomplice in the room with her, but there was no one; just Alex standing in the corner staring at the room.

The entire room had been turned upside down. Stuffing from the pillows lay scattered everywhere. The sheets and mattress were pulled off its base, and the tiny desk's drawers lay broken on the floor next to it.

"My room looks the same. The guy escaped through my window. Jumped both stories, would you believe it?"

"You saw him? Would you be able to describe him to the police?"

"No chance of that. He wore a mask, and besides, I only saw him from behind."

"What do you think he was looking for?" Alex asked.

"I don't know. Is anything missing?" replied Sam.

"No, I don't think so. I took all my notes and equipment with me. Even the camera's memory card. There was nothing here."

"We need to call the police, Alex. Might as well report our stolen vehicle."

"You're right. I'm calling the Commissioner-General directly on this one. My gut tells me this was no random attempted burglary."

M r. San Yeng-Pho and his small team of police officers arrived fifteen minutes later and met Sam and Alex in the lobby before going up to their rooms.

"Miss Hunt, please accept my apologies on behalf of the king and our prime minister. This matter is unacceptable, and we will do everything in our power to catch the ones who did this. Have you found anything missing?"

"Thank you, Mr. Yeng-Pho. No, nothing's missing from our rooms. However, our vehicle got stolen yesterday. We were out at the Nei Kar Slab Falls following up on a piece of information and when we went back to the Cruiser it was gone. We spent the night in the jungle, and when we got back here this morning, we walked into this."

"Nei Kar Slab Falls? Miss Hunt, there's a reason we refer to it as The Chasm of Death. It is a very dangerous place. Not only are the falls treacherous but the area still carries landmines, and there are many, many wild animals roaming that part of the jungle. Some even believe it is cursed. I am very happy and relieved to know you escaped it unscathed, but please don't go back there again."

Alex didn't comment. The police commissioner's plea was comforting, but not one she was likely to bend to as he clearly realized before he started up again. "Now, I will have my men comb the rooms for fingerprints and investigate if anyone heard or saw anything. As for your vehicle, Mr. Khen will take down all the details, and we will try to locate it, but I must be honest though, Miss Hunt, many revolutionary groups operate in that particular area on the Vietnam border, and the chance of us recovering the vehicle is extremely slim."

Alex unfolded her arms and placed it in her pants pockets. "Thank you for your concern, Commissioner, but we're simply following the clues. Wherever they may lead us."

Sam who stood quietly finally decided to add to the conversation before the commissioner could respond. "Ahem, Mr. Yeng-Pho, I doubt your men will find any fingerprints. The perp was wearing gloves."

"Gloves? How do you know, Dr. Quinn? You mean to tell me you saw him?"

"Indeed, just enough to see the guy jump my balcony and run across the street. He was wearing a black mask and black clothes from head to toe; actually just like the ninjas in the movies. I only caught sight of him from behind. He was a fast little bugger. I still don't know how he cleared two floors with such ease."

"Thank you Dr. Quinn. That is valuable information. I will have my team check the surveillance cameras from the street and see if we can identify anything else. In the meantime, I would suggest you stay at the hotel just to be safe until we clear the scene." The commissioner nodded and turned heading up the stairs to their rooms.

"Sir, one last thing, if I may?" Alex stopped him. "We would like to see the original police report and transcribes taken from the security guards at the temple, please? Could you have someone send it over?"

"With pleasure, Miss Hunt, anything to help you find our golden urn. I will also request that the hotel immediately move you to new rooms on the top floor. Once my men are finished processing your rooms, they'll have the porter take your luggage upstairs. Again, please accept our apologies and if you need anything else, don't hesitate."

And with that, Mr. Yeng-Pho delivered the instruction to the nearby hotel manager and followed him to their rooms up the stairs.

"Well then," Alex spun around. "Nothing for us to do now but wait. I am famished though. I guess we could go grab breakfast and recap on what we know thus far."

.   .   .

The he hotel lobby was a flurry of excited British and French tourists waiting for their shuttles to take them on excursions through the city. The full foyer meant that, thankfully, the breakfast room was quieting down as the last of them finished off. Alex and Sam found a quiet corner by the window overlooking the Tonle Sap River; a total contrast to the entrance of the hotel on the opposite side that was bustling with mopeds and street vendors. The ornate gold and red decor over the expansive windows afforded a certain regal atmosphere. Exactly what they needed. Calm. Neither said a word until they had finished their coffee and when their breakfasts arrived soon after. Alex pulled out her laptop and journal.

"Right. Let's see what we have this far, shall we? We know that there was a war over Buddha's relics. The Buddha died in Kushinagar, India who tried keeping all its relics for themselves. Then all havoc broke loose as seven other clans waged war against Kushinagar to claim possession of the relics."

"So how did it end up in Cambodia?" Sam asked.

"To keep the peace, it was divided across just about every Buddhist-majority country. Then, in 1957, The golden urn in question was gifted to the then ruler, king Sihanouk of Cambodia by the French, in commemoration of the 2,500th anniversary of Buddha's birth. It was enshrined in the mountain shrine here in Phnom Penh. That's where it had been ever since."

"Until now that is," Sam remarked through a mouthful of greasy bacon. "So essentially, any of the countries could have stolen it back. It could be anywhere. Didn't you say they divided nine hundred thousand strands of Buddha's hair?"

"If you can believe that, yes. What we do know for a fact is that, in total, eighty-four thousand shrines each received an urn containing different body parts of Buddha. So, if each of those shrines already have an urn, then my logic tells me they wouldn't need another, right?"

"I would agree," Sam said through another mouthful of food. "The urns are for religious ceremonial purposes alone. They wouldn't need to offer their respects to more than one."

Alex nodded as she took another sip of her coffee and stared pensively out the window.

Sam put another forkful of scrambled eggs in his mouth, "So wait, who verified what was inside each urn?" he asked.

"I would imagine the king, why?" Alex watched as Sam devoured his plate of food much like the bear stew he ate the night before.

"Well, it's just a thought, but why did we not see any reports from the supreme patriarch of the leading monastery? Why hasn't anyone spoken to the monks? From what I understand, they're the ones driving the Buddhism religion and are behind the people's protests to get the government off their behinds and investigate the theft of the golden urn in the first place. So the ritual sacrifices are for their purposes, mainly. They're also very involved in the politics of the country. Some monasteries even rebel against the government. It wasn't until they had these protests that the government decided to start their manhunt. What if they know something or worse, were somehow involved in the theft?"

Alex smiled with pride behind her coffee cup. The theory had never even entered her mind.

"You raise a valid point there, Dr. Quinn. I'm impressed. Everyone is a suspect until ruled out, right?"

Sam smiled. "Well let's see if I can impress you even more, Miss Hunt. The police file made no mention of any interviews with any of the monks at the stupa. We should see if we can get some information from the senior monks as to whether the urn was authentic, firstly, and secondly, find out if it indeed carried Buddha's remains. I can't imagine that only the king opened the urn and knew its contents. I think we should head up to the shrine and investigate it ourselves; see if perhaps the police missed anything. There should be a monk or two at the stupa too so we can start our questioning with them."

"Impressive indeed," Alex remarked before adding. "It might also be a good idea to trace the origin of the scroll the commissioner gave us. It led us nowhere thus far so I'm thinking it might be incomplete."

Alex nodded quietly in response as she ate her last piece of french toast.

"We need to figure out who turned our rooms upside down and what the guy thought he'd find. Any ideas?" Sam added.

Alex stared blankly out the window onto the river that stretched out on the other side of the busy street. She was calm, but Sam knew her well enough already to know something was up.

"Okay, out with it. What's bugging you?"

She wasn't surprised at all that he had caught onto her thoughts so didn't hesitate to answer.

"Well, I've been thinking about Ollie."

"Ollie! Why, have you discovered you in fact like the bloke?"

"Don't be silly! No! What I mean is that I've been wondering why he was out in the jungle when the bear cornered us. What was he doing there? Don't you find it strange that he'd be so far from his house at night?"

Sam thought about it for a second.

"Nope, not really. Perhaps he was just hunting for dinner and found us caught in the middle. Maybe a stroke of luck for him, I think."

"See, I don't agree. Ollie was too far off from his house. I don't think he was hunting. For one, he wouldn't have been able to carry any kill that far on his own, and then there was the gun strapped under his table. I don't think him meeting us there was a coincidence."

Sam sat back and giggled.

"So you think he broke into our rooms? Alex think about it. He's out there in the middle of the jungle all by himself. Of course he would need a gun to defend himself. Mr. Yeng-Pho said it himself. There are lots of guerrillas out there. Any of whom could slit his throat in the middle of the night. And why on earth would he be out there for us? Seriously, let it go. There's nothing sinister about the man. He was our Good Samaritan, and we'll probably never see him again."

"So you keep saying. But you told him what we're looking for remember? Perhaps he thought we had found it already and wanted a piece of the pie so he ransacked our rooms."

"Really? How did he do that if we left him at his cabin this morning? Unless the man can fly, I honestly doubt it, Alex. You're being paranoid."

"Fine, but I'm going to tell you 'I told you so' when the papaya hits the fan. Mark my words, Sam Quinn."

An hour later they had moved their belongings to the new upgraded rooms in the hotel and freshened up, rented a motorbike and were halfway to the mountain shrine in Oudong. The streets were busy. Organized chaos would be an apt way to describe the traffic as dozens of mopeds and motorbikes rambled the narrow streets. Many of these scooters carried entire families. Either on their laps or in the converted side carts resembling something more likened to a large go-kart covered by an umbrella.

The sidewalks were crammed with street vendors selling anything from clothing to fresh juice and chicken kebabs. Clusters of thick black power cords hung like Christmas decorations from telephone poles as it lined the streets in an untidy mess. Yet, each cable was neatly bundled and displayed a number or name tag with its classification.

Through all the chaos the commuters all seemed to drive in perfect harmony to each other. Like a well executed swan dance.

Sam miraculously managed to conform to the chaos and soon they reached the road that led out of the city toward the mountain shrine. They had barely approached the outskirts to the city when three motorcyclists gained on them from behind. Unlike the multitude of conventional mopeds they had just left behind in the city, these bikers rode on shiny black speed machines that stood out like sore thumbs. The bikers were dressed in black leather from head to toe. Their sleek helmets matching the attire in perfect cohesion and their visors tinted opaque with obvious intent to conceal their identities.

"Sam, these guys aren't friendlies. Go faster!"

Alex silently thanked Sam for insisting they rent a dirt bike instead of a moped to travel to the shrine. It was by no means as fast as the sport bikes these thugs were on but if they could get to the forest path they would certainly beat them on off-road mobility.

As if the bikers sensed their plan, two of them flanked their sides and one pulled in front of them, stinting their speed. Alex noticed the one to her right reaching for a gun from the back of his pants while the one to the left instantly followed his colleagues lead.

Adrenalin pushed through her veins and, much to her surprise, revealed exhilaration instead of fear. Her hand reached to where Sam's gun was still tucked in his waistband. Alex detested guns, probably out of it being totally unfamiliar to her, but her mind was now seized by the realization that this particular occasion called for it. She sensed these troublemakers meant business.

"Keep it steady, Sam. I have a plan," she spoke into his left ear while lifting his shirt and taking hold of the small revolver. Her instincts kicked in and she cocked back the hammer. With one smooth motion she kicked the biker's wheel to her right causing his bike to wobble and crash while she aimed the revolver and fired off a bullet into the biker to the left's engine. Sam moved out from behind the front biker and sped up next to him. Alex fired off another bullet into the wheel of his bike spinning it out of control as it went crashing off into the side of the road.

"Whoohoo! Alex you did it!" Sam exclaimed as he gathered speed to create a safe distance before pulling off to the side of the road. Once stationary, Alex jumped off the bike and ran for the bushes. Her stomach flipped upside down as she retched on the side of the road. The thought that she might have killed someone made her sick and she threw up until her stomach hurt. When she finally stopped to take a breath, she realized she still had the gun clasped in her shaking hand. She tossed it onto the road behind her. It landed against the motorbike's wheel with a loud clanking noise. Sam, who had walked a bit down the road to assess if the gang was still after them, flung around as the gun hit the metal and hurried toward her.

"Well there goes your breakfast little lady. You okay?"

Sam tucked the gun back behind his shirt. "That was some serious moves back there, Alex. I don't even want to know how you knew how to do that!" Sam rejoiced looking back onto the scene in the distance.

Alex wiped her mouth with the back of her hand and walked back to the bike.

"I have no idea who I was back there either! I killed three people, Sam, so no, I'm not okay."

"You think you killed them? You shot their bikes, Alex. I assure you they're just immobilized from a hard fall. At most a couple of broken bones and a concussion, but certainly not dead. Speaking of which, we should really get out of here before they catch up again."

Sam walked over to Alex and pulled her shaking body into his arms.

"You kicked their behinds, Alex. Some real action film stunts is what that was. I can't wait to tell your father when we get home. He won't believe it."

Sam was clearly impressed and his calm reassurance managed to bring a smile to Alex's face.

"I did kick butt, didn't I?" she smirked in triumph.

"I'd say! Hopefully they learned not to mess with you. Tough as nails you are, Alex Hunt. But I would suggest we hurry on up and head up to the stupa."

CHAPTER FOUR
Oudong, Cambodia

Tucked between lush trees and bushes, at the end of a long winding path up the side of the mountain, stood the sequence of stupas known as the Oudong Temple. The dirt bike maneuvered the trail with ease where it eventually ran dead at a small clearing in front of the ancient mystical complex.

"It's spectacular," Alex remarked as they dismounted under a shady tree. "The architecture is overwhelming."

"I would agree, it's fantastic, but all I see are millions of stairs to get to the top." Sam said with his usual jest.

Alex giggled. "Five hundred and nine steps to be exact and guess what? We have to climb all of them to get to the highest stupa which is where the golden urn was stolen from."

Sam didn't answer. Instead, he fixed his gaze on the white set of stairs in disbelief.

"See this as your Rocky Balboa moment," Alex teased.

"I'd say, Rocky Balboa amplified. As far as I recall those steps in Philadelphia were only seventy-two. These are seven times as many. But, if the reward delivers Stallone's muscles and hopefully a few clues to finding the urn, let's do it!"

The pair set off on the steep climb up the stairs stopping at the three dome-shaped stupas positioned in a row just below the fourth one, which was highest up the mountain. These stupas stood entirely separated from the one at the top making them accessible to tourists and open to the general public. There were groups of French students huddled with their sketchpads in front of the gold and ivory buildings. The fantastic ornate decorations of flowers and elephant heads on each stupa made for fascinating architectural inspiration. Each one was superbly distinguishable from the other and symbolized the three successions of Cambodian kings whose ashes were kept there.

A couple of tourists proudly posed for a photo in front of the enormous Buddha statue while a group of four devotees sat kneeled in prayer in front of a small shrine of burning incense.

"There's this deep sense of spirituality up here, isn't there Sam? Regardless of whether you're a Buddhist or not, you feel such peace and sanctity." Alex remarked as she took several photos of the shrine and ceremonial relics behind the glass windows.

"To think most of this is the surviving remains of the former royal capital city before it moved to Phnom Penh. The Khmer Rouge attacked and destroyed practically everything when they ruled between 1975 and 1979. It was devastating. Apparently, almost two million Cambodians died of starvation, execution, disease or being overworked. It was one of the biggest genocides in Eastern history. All because of social power."

"And there she is. Alex Hunt, remarkable historian. How do you even know all this stuff? I've never even heard of the Khmer Rouge," Sam said in awe of her knowledge.

"School was a very lonely place for me, Sam. I didn't have any friends. I never really had the time to make any because we were always traveling. So all I did was find a quiet corner and read books. I could escape the rejection and hurt of not fitting in with a book. History has always been my favorite topic. I find it fascinating. Real life events that took place all over the world. Are you kidding me? It's incredible. Besides, I guess, secretly I aimed to make sure I always went with my parents on their travels. If I knew more than they did, well then they'd find a reason to take me with them, and I wouldn't have to stay behind."

"Makes perfect sense. So who were these Khmer Rouge people?" Sam asked.

"It was a communist movement whose sole motive was to eliminate an entire social order in the country. Rouge is French for Red, which signified the bloodshed during their murderous onslaught. They were aggressive and vicious. But in early 1979 Vietnamese troops invaded Cambodia and captured Phnom Penh. They established a moderate Communist government, and the Khmer Rouge retreated back into the jungle. So they're still out there with the motivation to strike at any time whenever a new insurgent swoops in. Most of the older generation who lived through the Rouge walk on eggshells. They live in daily fear of them returning."

"That's brutal," Sam remarked. "Oh, that reminds me. The biker had a tattoo on the back of his neck. It was a black scorpion. Do you think that means anything?"

"A scorpion? It could mean something, I'm sure. I just wouldn't know what. I do know that the Cambodians are very superstitious and they believe in magic tattoos in strategic places on their bodies. The tigers usually mean they're fighters or in a fight club of some sorts but I've never heard of people getting scorpion tattoos."

"It might mean nothing, but you never know. I only caught sight of the thug's neck because he was in front of us," said Sam.

"Well, we'll ask around just in case. If those guys were of the same gang as the one who burgled our rooms, then something's up. I still don't know why they're after us."

"Those three back there meant business, Alex. They're after something, that's certain. Perhaps they think we have found the urn already. Speaking of, let's get up to the top stupa and see if something stands out in the shrine."

Another multitude of steps further up the mountain brought them to the highest stupa that was taped off with bright orange police tape. As they approached the dome, two security guards flung their rifles over their shoulders and pointed it at them, stopping both Sam and Alex dead in their tracks.

"No tourist allow," one of them said in broken English.

Sam's hands went up in the air as Alex attempted to reach into her backpack to pull the commissioner's authorization letter out. This spooked one of the guards and immediately sent him into an aggressive response thinking she was trying to pull out a gun. The guard raised his rifle and aimed it directly at her face while shouting several commands in Mandarin.

Immediately Alex dropped her backpack and threw her arms into the air.

"Non, Non, S'il Vous plaît! Nous avons la permission du commissaire!" she tried explaining in French hoping her lack of speaking mandarin wouldn't aggravate the situation. The guard stood his ground and kept the rifle pointed at them. Sam found it hard to swallow the anxious dry spot that sat wedged in the back of his throat as he nervously looked at Alex. She repeated the phrase again in desperation to get through to the guards.

The more mature guard who seemed to be in charge answered back in french asking for the permission document she claimed she had. His hand gripped his rifle tighter while still pointing it at her face in anticipation of danger but allowed Alex to reach into her backpack. Alex cautiously retrieved the official letter stamped by Mr. San Yeng-Pho granting them permission to enter the stupa. The guard scanned it over and handed it back with a polite apology, permitting them to pass as if nothing had happened.

The commissioner's high rank clearly did the trick.

"Now that was a close call," a relieved Sam said as they pushed past the guards up the last flight of stairs. "Is it my imagination or did they seem super aggressive?"

"I think the entire country is on tenterhooks with the theft of the urn, Sam. The longer it takes to find it, the more on edge they all are," Alex answered while taking her shoes off signaling for Sam to do the same. The large wooden, hand-carved door to the stupa was heavy and called for both of them needing to lean into it to push it open. The exquisite carvings in itself told an ancient story of a historical wonder; a city steeped in tradition and spirituality, but rife with political undercurrents, fear, and blood spill.

T he sacred building was deathly quiet inside with not a soul in sight. A few lit candles burned at the foot of the shrine in the center of the double volume building. Orange police tape surrounded the glassed chamber and a perfect circular hole in the glass window on the other end proved evidence that a crime was recently committed.

Several garlands of fresh flowers decorated the floor all around the shrine and the smell of incense permeated the air. Smaller Buddha statues surrounded the square platform where the urn was once displayed.

"Apart from the urn, it doesn't look like anything is out of the ordinary. Judging from the entry point, I'd say these were professional burglars," Alex commented as she circled the shrine.

"I'd agree, Watson," Sam mocked with a sideways glance.

"Watson! You mean Sherlock. What makes you think I'm your sidekick? Might I remind you that I saved your behind back there," Alex joked back.

"Okay, okay, you win. Can't argue with that one. You were saying?" Sam spurred Alex on.

"Well," Alex continued, "as I was saying, my guess is, the burglars used a diamond cutter and suction pad. Extremely precise with no noise disturbance; which explains why the dogs were the only detectors. This theft wasn't just a common burglary."

Alex noticed as Sam stared at her in surprise. "And you know this how?" he asked.

"My Dad. He's a huge James Bond fan," Alex replied flippantly.

"Ahem, may I be of any assistance?" A soft male voice spoke behind them. The monk bowed in the customary prayerful greeting as they both turned around to face him, prompting them to bow in response.

"Choum Reap Sur, Bhante," Alex greeted promptly in his native language as a sign of respect to the elder monk. "I am Alex Hunt, and this is Sam Quinn. We have been commissioned by your king to recover the stolen golden urn."

The senior monk's gaze lingered on their faces for a few seconds before he politely gestured for them to follow him through a small doorway on the other end of the large room. Sam, being over six feet tall, stooped over to get through the tiny space, which then opened up into a generous room with a vaulted roof. The ceilings were elaborately decorated with gold flowers. It was jaw dropping.

"Wow!" Sam sounded off.

"Shh, you can't speak in here," Alex whispered. "It's the holiest most sacred place in the entire temple. This is where the monks gather for meditation and teaching," she proceeded in a muted tone.

Again Sam shook his head in disbelief of her considerable knowledge of the culture. As far as he knew, she had never been inside a Buddhist temple before and yet she knew precisely how to greet them and what not to do.

Up ahead at the very far end of the hall, a small group of monks sat cross-legged on small purple mats on the floor. Their bright saffron robes along with dozens of lit candles around them illuminated the room to a radiant glow. Facing them sat a much older monk on a raised pedestal reading from an odd looking sheet.

The senior monk signaled for Alex and Sam to sit at the back of the group and placed his finger on his mouth instructing them to be silent. Alex was in awe while Sam shuffled several times in an uncomfortable attempt to cross his long legs. Civilians are never permitted to sit in on teachings so this was an exceptional honor to be a part of. Alex couldn't understand a single word the monk uttered, but somehow, her mind became a dull space of extreme calm. She could feel herself gradually losing awareness of Sam who eventually settled on one leg stretched out in front of him and the other half tucked underneath. She closed her eyes and listened to the soothing murmured teaching. Apart from the Buddhist priest's voice, one could hear a pin drop. She had no idea how long she sat in her tranced state, but it was only when the priest sounded a chiming bell, and the students got to their feet, that she opened her eyes again.

"Welcome back sleeping beauty," Sam whispered close to her ear.

"Did I fall asleep?" an embarrassed Alex replied.

"Not sure, you were definitely off somewhere other than here. You might want to wipe the drool off your chin."

Appalled Alex's hand shot up to her face as she vigorously wiped her chin with her scarf that covered her head and shoulders.

Sam chuckled. "Relax Princess. I was just teasing. You're as pretty as the flowers on this ceiling."

"Ha-ha very funny Mr. Pretzel," she bit back jumping to her feet while Sam unknotted his now numbed legs."

Moments later the senior monk appeared next to them and ushered the pair in front of the priest. As they exchanged greetings, Alex caught sight of the unusual looking sheet he had been reading from on the table beside them. There were stacks of similar sheets next to it. The priest spoke to the senior monk in mandarin who promptly translated accordingly. "Miss Hunt, my honorable priest invites you to take a closer look."

Alex practically jumped out of her skin with excitement. "Really? I would be honored," she exclaimed dropping her head toward the priest again.

"What are they?"

"They are ancient writings of Buddha's teachings, Miss Hunt. They were written more than a thousand years ago."

"Phenomenal, what is this paper?" Alex asked in awe.

"It is a fusion of banana leaf and rice paper. The ink is liquid gold."

"No way!" Sam exclaimed. "Real gold ink?"

"Precisely Dr. Quinn. It is ancient and was reserved for sacred texts only."

The exquisite beauty of the sheets of banana leaf writings had Alex and Sam both mesmerized.

"What does it say?" she asked.

The monk picked up one of the sheets and started translating.

> May I think of every living being
> As more precious than a wish giving gem
> For reaching the ultimate goal,
> And so always hold them dear.
>
> When I'm with another, wherever we are,
> May I see myself as the lowest.
> May I hold the other as the highest,
> From the bottom of my heart.
>
> As I go through the day may I watch my mind,
> To see if a negative thought has come;
> If it does May I stop it right there, with force,
> Since it hurts others and myself.

"How unbelievably profound. And this is what today's teaching was about? Humility and kindness?" an equally stunned Sam asked.

The senior monk nodded and then placed the sheet back on the rest of the stack. On top of the sheaf, he proceeded to position a similarly shaped piece of wood and fastened strips of cloth around the pile in a tight bow before wrapping it up in a cutting of fabric.

"It's a book," Alex says excitedly. "A magnificently bound book of banana leaf pages and wooden book covers all wrapped up in a neat parcel. Absolutely astonishing."

Sam turned to the monks and bowed prayerfully in gratitude, "Thank you for this honor. This was truly the most remarkable artifact I have ever seen."

A still gawking Alex followed suit, bending at the waist several times.

"I think he knows how appreciative you are, Alex. One bow usually does it," Sam said surreptitiously behind his palms that were still held together in front of his chest.

"Oh yes-yes of course. Ahem," Alex cleared her throat switching to a more business-like tone. "Venerable, thank you for this honor. We need your assistance if you don't mind?"

The priest nodded.

"We have been tasked to recover the golden urn. Forgive me for asking, but there are rumors that the stolen urn was a counter-feit. Would you be able to dispel this by any chance?"

Alex felt her stomach somersault as she waited for the senior monk to translate her question; anticipating he would be highly offended at her cheeky question. There was a long silent pause before the priest responded with a reply that caught them both off guard. "A pure heart cannot derail the sanctity of his holi-ness. For an object remains cold and without a soul, but the heart of a believer conquers all."

And with that, the priest bowed and slipped out through another small door behind him.

The senior monk waited patiently for them to respond but neither Sam nor Alex spoke immediately in the wake of his words.

"Oh don't mind him, Sheila. The old bat always speaks in parables."

"Ollie! Wh—what are YOU doing here?"

"G'day Mate," ignoring Alex's question with a firm pat on Sam's back after which he turned to the senior monk and hugged him as if he were family.

"Nice to see you again, Marut," the monk responded.

"Marut? Who on earth is Marut?" a still dumbstruck Alex uttered.

"Ah, Sheila, no need to look so surprised. Roshi and I go way back. We're practically brothers. Now, what brings the two of you here, huh?"

There was no way on earth Alex was going to give him the satisfaction of a truthful answer. Quick on her feet, she replied with a simple, "Nothing, just taking in some tourist attractions, that's all."

Alex threw Sam a warning look who, on the other hand, could spill the beans to his new 'friend' very easily. Instead, he caught her stare and refrained from speaking. But it was evident Ollie didn't believe a word she said when he quickly switched to converse with the monk in perfect mandarin. Moments later Ollie stood back with a grin so wide it looked as if the corners of his mouth were going to tear open.

"Well, why didn't you just say so, Sheila? I told you two lovebirds I could help, and I know just the man to help us."

"'Us'? Oh no, Ollie or Marut or whatever you call yourself. There's no 'US' in this equation, thank you. This is a Hunt team expedition. You are hardly an expert on this subject!"

"Shh, let's not get upset in here, Sheila. This is a holy place. Let's take it outside, before you lift the rafters." Ollie pushed all her buttons with deliberate intent, and he relished in it.

It just about took all her self-control not to slap Ollie across the face. She cursed the man in her thoughts for letting him crawl under her skin.

"He's right, Alex, let's go. We don't want to cause a commotion." Sam placed a firm hand on her elbow and ushered her toward the door and outside the stupa.

"Let go of my arm, Sam! I'm not a child. What the heck is he doing here? I'm telling you, this guy is as slippery as those eels you buy at the night market. He's not all he says he is, and why the heck are you siding with him?" Alex couldn't decide if she was angry at Ollie or angry at Sam for supporting Ollie with his exaggerated patriotism toward him. She spun around toward the stairs, "I'm leaving. I don't have time for this snake's antics."

"Alex, wait!" Sam shouted after her. "Let's at least hear what the guy has to say. Maybe he can help. He certainly seems to know his way around. Let's use him to our advantage to further our quest. It can't hurt. Come on, five minutes, then we leave okay?"

Alex wasn't sure why Ollie crept under her skin the way he did. All she knew was to trust her instincts. As she stood arms crossed outside the stupa listening to Sam trying to convince her, she recalled something her Dad once taught her.

Keep your friends close and your enemies closer

Sam is right. They were there to find out more about the urn and Ollie did speak mandarin, so it made sense to use him to their advantage. She kicked a pebble down the ivory stone staircase.

"Fine" she replied finally. "But I'm out of here if he calls me Sheila again, do you hear me, Sam Quinn?"

"Agreed."

Ollie was still talking to the senior monk as they walked back into the temple room.

"Ah, so you decided you need my help after all." Ollie said with a sheepish grin on his face.

"Oh don't flatter yourself. We have a job to do, so get on with it. Who's this *guy* that can help us?" Alex wasn't about to let Ollie's obnoxious ego derail her. She'd play ball but only for the sake of their quest.

"Ahem," Sam cut in. "Ollie, what Alex meant to say is that we would appreciate any assistance in the matter? We're trying to establish if indeed the stolen urn was authentic. If it wasn't it means that the original relic is still out there somewhere."

Ollie spotted Alex's stern face. This was one female who wasn't about to let him mess with her. This was his single chance if he were to find what he's after. He looked her square in the eye, "I will offer you whatever assistance you might need. Just say the word, Alex."

Alex wasn't prepared for his comment at all. 'Alex.' The man hasn't once referred to her as anything other than Sheila. Could it be that she has won this silent battle of authority against him? Perhaps standing next to Roshi in a sacred temple somehow penetrated his heart with compassion. No, he wasn't to be trusted. Wolf in sheep's clothing is what he was. She pushed her chin out and pulled back her shoulders. "Why don't you start by taking us to whomever you were referring to earlier? Who do you know that could help us find the original urn?"

Ollie shifted and propped his one hand on his hip whilst whacking his hat against his thigh with the other. "Now, I never said he'd find you the original urn. Heck, we don't even know if the stolen urn was a fake or not."

Alex felt her hands ball into a fist. Something both Ollie and Sam noticed instantly, so Sam interjected calmly. "But this guy you speak of can somehow shed some light if indeed this was an authentic relic, correct?"

"Bloody oath, Mate. If anyone has the answer it will be my guy Charlie." Ollie was filled with pride as if he just bragged about his best friend.

Roshi nodded in agreement, "Okay, we go?"

Sam clapped his hands together like a car salesman who just concluded a deal. "We go, yes. No time like the present."

"I guess I don't have a choice in the matter, do I?" Alex said still not convinced she should trust Ollie.

CHAPTER FIVE

O llie and Roshi led the way down the stairs and beyond the ever-mounding group of tourists. At the foot of the flight of stairs Roshi veered to the right between the large trees on the edge of the forest. As the mid day sun beat down hard on them, the small party headed east down the mountain between dense trees and shrubs before finally coming to a stop in front of a giant tree. Its thick roots were intertwined vertically like an impenetrable nest of vines reaching up into the heavens. It was the tallest tree they had ever seen. Lush green leaves poked through the coiled vines that seemed to grow on forever. There was something so majestic about it. The sun beamed through the dense leafy canopy above, illuminating and exalting it to its full glory.

"Ain't it something, mates?" Ollie asked boastfully as he watched Alex and Sam's thunderstruck faces.

"Something? It's the most spectacular thing I've ever seen!" Sam exclaimed.

Alex's mouth was still open in awe of this natural wonder that stood tall and strong in front of her. So much so that she completely lost focus of the supposed 'guy' Ollie said he was taking them to. "How old is it?" She finally asked.

"Many, many centuries, Miss Hunt," Roshi answered. "But what you are about to discover has never been made known to the lay man. It is sacred and our monastery's best kept secret. You must vow to never reveal this to anyone."

Sam and Alex nodded in unison. Their individual heartbeats resounded loudly in their ears as they glanced at each other with an unspoken promise of something completely unknown to them. Whatever Roshi wanted to show them alluded to an ancient mystery that was about to unfold before their very eyes.

Roshi looked to Ollie for a final 'are you sure about this?' to which Ollie confidently nodded his approval in response. The monk took several paces to the left and pulled away a curtain of green shrubbery. There behind the mass of leaves was a hand-carved wooden door encased between solid stone walls and columns. Ancient symbols were etched out in the wood and stone. A veil of light green moss covered the stone in a thick crust which further revealed with certitude that this entrance was at least several hundred years old.

"What is this place?" Alex asked.

Ollie's face lit up with impish glee in the knowledge that she would have never found this on her own. "It's a hidden entrance to an ancient temple that no one except the monks who use it, knows of."

An equally stunned Sam moved toward it and touched the carvings on the door. "And you know of this how exactly?" he asked.

Alex was so enamored of the scene before her that she never stopped to think how Ollie came to know of the secret passage until Sam mentioned it. "Good point. If this isn't known to anyone other than the monks, how come you know about it?" She pushed for an answer.

Ollie's face turned to a sheepish grin before he flippantly answered, "Oh, it's a long story, Sheila. Like I said, Roshi and I go way back."

The question hung unanswered in the air as Ollie pushed the heavy door ajar. "Well, what do you say we go inside?" Ollie deliberately deflected from their question. "After you my friend," Ollie ushered Roshi through the doorway first.

It was cool and slightly damp inside with hundreds of candles lining the floor of the narrow passage.

"Unbelievable," Alex whispered under her breath as she struggled to contain herself. The secret passage was deadly quiet apart from the light shuffling of their feet along the terracotta tiled floor.

The walls of the secret tunnel were constructed with narrow clay bricks that had crumbled in some places and left behind compacted red sand cavities. The rounded roof was low and offered very little headroom for Sam who was as in awe as Alex. A musty earthy smell tainted with only the faintest odor of burning candles lay thick in the air.

Alex glanced back at Sam with a mischievous smile bursting with excitement, to which Sam equally excitedly mouthed, "I know!" in response.

Alex found herself bursting with questions and could no longer contain her excitement. "Roshi, how old is this tunnel?"

Roshi stopped abruptly and turned facing Alex before ever so softly answering, "It dates back to the 12th century, Miss Hunt, but please, we cannot speak a word inside these tunnels, and especially when we get to the Wat. It is very sacred and only the holiest of monks live here. They are vowed to silence so you may not speak at all."

Alex bowed in apology even though the gesture was completely unfitting to the situation. But Roshi bowed back and continued leading them through the remarkable tunnel. They were thoroughly awestruck by the beauty of the formation and the profound knowledge of walking through a monk-built underground tunnel that was almost ten centuries old, took their breaths away. The anticipation mounted as they continued through the subterranean tunnel that turned several corners first before eventually ending in front of a sandstone carved Buddha statue. At its feet were dozens of candles burning incense and small golden sacrificial urns that most likely contained food. The small chamber was completely closed off. There were no windows or doors.

Roshi turned around and handed them each an unlit candle.

"We have to pay our respects first."

Ollie took a candle without any hesitation and went onto his knees in front of the statue. Alex and Sam watched as a usually cocky Ollie transformed into a melancholy being in front of their very eyes. His usual flippant, happy-go-lucky demeanor was instantly replaced by a deep sadness that didn't quite match up to the Ollie they have come to know. Alex was certain she saw him tear up but chose to conceal her observation from him. She realized in that moment, that whatever first impressions she might have had about him was nothing but a smokescreen. There was more to this man than what met the eye. So she silently knelt down beside him.

Several minutes later, Roshi rose and walked over to the wall that flanked the statue and one by one they too rose and joined him.

"Now what?" Alex whispered to the group before directing her attention to Ollie. "Where do we find this man you said can help us? I thought you said there were other monks here, but we're completely closed off inside this chamber."

Ollie smiled. "Patience is a virtue, Sheila," and winked at Roshi.

Had it not been for Alex's earlier observation she would have snapped back at him. Instead, she rolled her eyes and looked questioningly at Roshi who turned and lifted a single brick from the wall. Instantly a small doorway receded into the wall and slid behind the stone structure to open up to another secret tunnel.

"Fascinating!" Alex and Sam gasped almost simultaneously. Roshi placed his forefinger on his mouth reminding them not to speak, and proceeded through the opening in the wall. Once he passed through he pulled out another brick from the inside, closing the stone door behind them.

Alex felt weak with excitement. Her heart was beating so fast she thought it was going to propel her into a sprint to the end of the mysterious tunnel. Overwhelmed with emotion she was close to tears. Never, in all her years, had she ever had the privilege of exploring an underground secret tunnel to a centuries old monastery. In the faint candlelight, she spotted that even the ever dependable and contained Sam could barely hold together his excitement. It was an experience the two of them would never forget.

T he soft glow of Roshi's candle illuminated the tunnel that was much narrower than the preceding one, forcing them to walk in a single file. It was also far more unrefined. The bricks were extremely porous and, unlike the first tunnel, grey in color with large cavities throughout the walls. The floor was vastly different too. Instead, the beautiful terracotta tiles had made way for an uneven, patchy stone floor that showed significant signs of deterioration in several places. Then there was the pungent smell so strong it likened to that of a sewage. Their footsteps echoed through the hollow space as the small group silently moved through the tunnel; echoing as if they were inside a cave.

It wasn't long before they reached a wooden door that Roshi opened with the utmost care so as to not make a noise. Remarkably there wasn't the slightest squeak from any of the hinges, as one might have expected of a door exposed to so much damp. Alex found herself wondering if it was even safe to be so deeply buried underground.

The door opened up to a small rounded chamber with a set of sandstone stairs. A bright beam of sunlight shone from the top of the stairs. The sigh of relief that came from Sam who had to walk bent over the entire way, was extremely amusing and Alex had to restrain herself from exploding into laughter. Though she didn't have to walk hunched like he did, confined underground spaces didn't agree with her much. She was as relieved as Sam was to finally reach the top of the stairs that opened to a magnificent courtyard filled with lush gardens and trees. Several monks clad in their bright saffron robes were scattered throughout the gardens. Some were tending to the shrubs while others were seated on ancient stone benches that stood interspersed between the large shady trees. No one spoke a word. It was deathly silent apart from the tranquil sound of the water in the large fountain next to the lily pad fishpond.

The ambience held a magnificent reverence for their religion, one that was almost palpable.

Large square columns linked with scalloped wooden fringes hedged in the courtyard. The monks were completely undisturbed by their presence as Roshi continued leading the small party through the courtyard to the double volume corridors that appeared just beyond the columns. It was majestic to say the least. In total contradiction to Sam and Alex, both Ollie and Roshi's heads were bowed as they moved silently through the monastery. Just as Alex and Sam thought they had seen all magnificence there is to discover, they were ushered into a closed room bursting with rich colors of magenta, mustard and saffron. The tiled floor was covered with a large magenta pink rug upon which about a dozen young boys sat cross-legged in prayer. Their bright orange clothing lay in stark contrast to the rug and the circular burgundy and gold pillars held the elevated ceiling in place above their heads.

An enormous gold encrusted Buddha sat cross-legged in front of the boys. Its eyes were open as if it were looking down at them in commendation. By its feet were hand-painted blue and white porcelain vases filled with the brightly colored flowers from the courtyard garden. Several picture-frames with photographs of senior monks stood proudly in between. You could hear a pin drop. Although these boys ranged in age from about eight to fourteen, not one of them fidgeted or made a single noise. Instead, they practiced a discipline so intense that not even the small party's movement to the door on the other side of the room distracted them.

The adjoining room was similar in size and embellished with bursts of gold. In total contrast, to the bold colors of the boys' meditation room, it displayed muted tones of ivory and white. The Buddha statue in the front of the room was made from white marble stone and polished to a shiny splendor. This time they were alone in the room. Roshi closed the door behind them and signaled for them to take a seat on the ivory cushions on the floor in front of the Buddha before disappearing through a corridor leading out from the room.

Alex didn't waste any time. Naturally a bit of a talker, being in silence deemed a real challenge, especially when her head was exploding with questions.

"Psst, Ollie," she whispered. "What's going on? Who is this man you said would help us? How is he supposed to help us if he can't speak?"

Ollie whispered back, "Ever heard of the board-game charades? They love it." Sam and Ollie broke into a giggle muffled behind their palms.

"Ha-ha! Very funny," Alex whispered back before joining in the restrained laughter.

It seemed the silence set them off into a delirious stupor as they held their tummies aching with inward laughter.

"How do they do it?" an out of breath Sam eventually asked. "I could not live a day without hearing Alex speak," folding double and setting them all off again.

"Shh, we need to get it together if we want to get a meeting with the Supreme Patriarch."

Instantly Alex jerked upright and stopped laughing. "The Supreme Patriarch? Isn't he the highest ranked monk in the Monastery?"

"Thought that might catch your attention, Sheila. Jokes aside, he's a hundred and two years old. He was in his sixties when the urn was gifted to the king. He preceded over the ceremony and placed the urn in the shrine."

"You had better not be messing with me, Ollie. This is serious."

"Alexandra, does it look like I'm lying to you? I told you I would help you, didn't I? That's what I'm doing, helping."

Sam looked perplexed. "If you don't mind me asking, Ollie, why? What's in it for you?"

It was a question Alex had been aching to ask, and she was relieved to know that Sam wasn't as trusting of Ollie as she might have thought.

Much to Ollie's delight, Roshi entered the room and beckoned for them to follow him. Without a second's hesitation, Ollie jumped up and walked over to where Roshi was already heading down the corridor.

"What did I tell you, Sam? He's up to no good," Alex whispered to Sam as she got up and hastened toward the corridor.

"I think you might be right, Alex," Sam whispered back, close on her heels. "He's not being honest with us, but for now, let's just keep an eye on him, okay?"

Roshi shot a stern look their way to silence them as they continued down the long corridor and down a set of stairs before stopping in the middle of the passage.

"We rest for tonight. Miss Hunt, this is your room. Dr. Quinn, this is yours," pointing to two doors opposite from one another. "Tomorrow morning we will meet the venerable Patriarch."

And with that he and Ollie disappeared back up the corridor and up the stairs.

"What on earth? Why is Ollie going with him?" Alex whispered.

"Who knows? They go way back, remember? Maybe he gets a special room."

Sam's sarcasm was sincere and not in jest to tease her. Had he finally seen what Alex had seen in Ollie?

"Okay, well I guess we have no choice do we? Must say I'm ravenous," Alex whispered.

"Yup, I'd give a tooth for some bear stew but something tells me we're going to bed hungry," Sam responded.

"If I have my facts right, the monks don't eat after midday and they're not allowed to hoard food, so it's very likely we're not going to eat before morning."

Sam pondered over Alex's utterance. "Okay, I'm just putting it out there. I'm starving. We haven't eaten anything since breakfast, which, as I recall you deposited on the side of the road. What do you say we go do a bit of *exploring* so to speak and find the kitchen? There has to be something somewhere for us to eat."

Alex who had already opened her door to her small bedroom, turned around, shocked at his suggestion. "Have you lost your mind, Sam Quinn? In case you haven't noticed, we are in a monastery and we're supposed to be in our rooms, not wandering about unattended. What if we get caught?"

She looked up and down the corridor for anyone who might have overheard his suggestion.

"Oh come on, Alex, live a little. In fact, if I don't get any food right now I might not live at all."

Alex couldn't argue. Her rumbling stomach wouldn't allow for her to sleep at all. "Okay, but we're not hanging about any longer than what's necessary. Agreed?"

A delighted Sam nodded enthusiastically, "Absolutely, now let's get on with it before I faint."

The famished pair shuffled along the passage wall like thieves in the night. Alex who rarely broke any rules, nervously clung to Sam whilst she frequently looked behind her. Sam, on the other hand, was like a naughty school boy; exhilarated by the notion of sneaking around in a monastery.

As luck would have it, the passage opened up into a spacious mess hall with rows and rows of wooden tables and benches.

Large wooded doors opened up to an adjoining garden bursting with fresh vegetables and herbs. There was not a monk in sight.

"Oh great! We hit the mother load," Sam exclaimed sarcastically.

"Shh! Do you want us to get caught?" Alex hushed him.

There wasn't a monk in sight but their voices echoed through the expansive room making it very difficult not to be heard.

"I'm sorry, but I'm not the vegetable type, you know? I'm more of a meat and potatoes guy," he whispered back as he rummaged through the stacked baskets at the doorway to the garden.

"Monks don't eat much meat, Sam. It's highly unlikely we'll find anything of substance at all. We have carrots and tomatoes, it's better than nothing. Let's go!" Alex started to panic. There was no way she'd want to be thrown out and jeopardize a meeting with the Supreme Patriarch.

But Sam's stomach was clearly winning the battle. He was already at the far end of the hall when Alex returned with a small harvest of fresh produce from the garden.

"What the heck, Sam? We need to get out of here."

A force far greater than the opportunity to meet a hundred-and-two-year-old monk possessed Sam. The canteen worktop harbored several baskets underneath, which Sam searched frantically.

"Yes!" he cried out. "Bread!"

"For goodness' sake, Sam. Keep it down. Grab it and let's go."

With a full supply of groceries, the two hurriedly set off down the passage and ducked into Alex's room. Sam didn't waste any time. He fell down on the thin mattress on the floor and bit off a large chunk from the loaf of bread.

"This is the best bread I've ever tasted," uttering groans of satisfaction while chomping off another large piece.

"You sure you don't want to add some cheese?" Alex teased.

"If this were European monks we'd have had some good Tuscan vino to add to the cheese," he joked back.

CHAPTER SIX

A loud bell woke them at 4 a.m. the next morning. Sam came stumbling half-asleep into Alex's room, arching his back in an attempt to click his vertebrae back into place after sleeping on the hard floor. Alex sat up in bed fumbling with her watch to read the time.

"Oh, you've got to be kidding me. The sun's not even up yet," she groaned pulling the blanket over her head.

Moments later the monks sent a choir of chanting morning prayers through the crisp morning air causing Alex to pull the saffron blanket even tighter over her head.

"Rise and shine sleeping beauty. Think of it this way. We should hopefully get a decent breakfast. Last night's pilferage barely touched sides."

She had to admit. Sam had a naughty streak in him she had never seen before. She thoroughly enjoyed their secret rendezvous to the kitchen, but she woke up ravenous this morning.

"I don't think it will be pancakes and bacon, Sam. But I'll promise you this much. If Ollie is messing us around, I will personally wring his neck."

"Oh, I'll hold him down for you, Alex. My back is killing me after sleeping on that thin little mattress on the floor. We had better walk off here today with a decent clue to that urn or else."

Alex giggled. Sam wasn't a rough-and-tumble kind of guy. "Yeah yeah tough guy, perhaps we should get ready before these monks find you in my quarters."

Twenty minutes later, the chanting had stopped and Roshi was waiting in the corridor outside their rooms. Ollie was nowhere in sight.

"Morning," Alex mouthed to Roshi not sure if she was allowed to speak or not and tapped on Sam's door to join them.

Walking into the eating hall, Sam threw Alex a naughty smile. She was equally amused. But, unlike the bare dining mess the night before, the eating hall was packed to the rafters with cheery monks in bubbling conversation over hearty bowls of soup. Ollie sat in the middle of the room amidst a small group of men who greatly enjoyed his Aussie chatter. The man was noticeably the center of attention. A baffled Alex and Sam exchanged surprised expressions as they made their way to his table.

"G'day Mates. What took you so long? You almost missed the most important meal of the day. Get some nosh and eat up. Our meeting is in fifteen minutes."

It had just gone 4:40 a.m.

"Have these people all lost their minds?" a stunned Alex whispered to Sam who nudged her by the elbow toward the server where the chef stood dishing up steaming bowls of watery vegetable broth and bread. Sam's disappointment was very evident as he grumpily tucked into his nosh, consequently sending Alex into an uncontrollable giggle. They whisked through their morning meal and finished just in time for Ollie to gesture that it was now time for their meeting.

Alex found herself nervously fidgeting with her headscarf in anticipation of their meeting; delighted that a game of charades was seemingly off the table if the cheery banter of the monks at breakfast were anything to go by.

The lengthy informal tour through the monastery deposited them on the opposite wing of the establishment that was even more lavishly decorated. It was unquestionably set aside for the more prominent members of the community.

"Wait here please," Roshi ordered as they entered a modest foyer and then disappeared behind a small red door.

Unlike the rest of the cloister, this room didn't have the same poignant smell of incense. It was plainly furnished with six red ottomans spaced in rows of three opposite from each other. Alex's eyes sparkled in anticipation as she paced the tiny room. It wasn't often a lay person had the honor of meeting the great Supreme Patriarch of the Buddhist community in South-East Asia. He was practically the Dalai Lama or Buddha himself. She bit her thumbnail. A habit she still had even though her agoraphobia was almost non-existent of late.

"Chill out Sheila. He won't bite," Ollie snickered.

"And how would you know exactly?" Alex bit back.

"Well he hasn't any teeth left for one and he is hands down the wisest man I've ever met."

Ollie's flippant declaration had Alex and Sam respond in complete unison, "You've met him?"

Throwing his hands in the air, Ollie responded. "Whoa cobbers, don't look so surprised. Of course I've met him. I told you, these guys are like family to me."

As if on cue to help Ollie evade further questions, Roshi popped his head out from behind the red door and ushered them in. The dazed pair hastily followed Roshi into a poorly lit room where the supreme monk sat in a gold and red armchair. Standing slightly behind him to his right with his eyes staring at his feet was a younger monk whom they presumed was his caregiver.

Roshi and Ollie hurried over and sat cross-legged in front of him on the floor, so Alex and Sam hastily followed suit. The elderly man didn't look a day over eighty until his friendly face softened into a broad smile to reveal glistening pink gums instead of teeth. His face lit up like a candle when he saw Ollie and greeted him enthusiastically in Mandarin. Ollie responded with equal glee as if it were his father. The confusion on Alex's face must have been evident, for seconds later, the patriarch's attention moved to Alex and Sam who silently sat watching the reunion. Ollie and Roshi both laughed in response to something he said after which Ollie turned to Alex.

"He wants to know if you think he bites that you look so scared."

Every cell in her being wanted to lash out at Ollie for making fun of her, but she couldn't. Instead, she pushed her chin up and forced her sweetest smile without responding. Ollie's face dropped. He was unmistakably convinced she would participate in his sick little game and bite back with some snide remark. An amused Sam cleared his throat in an attempt to bring them both back to matters at hand. Roshi caught on and swiftly addressed the guru.

The room went quiet before the senior monk finally looked at Alex and Sam and said, "I understand you are looking for the urn?"

Alex and Sam turned to each other surprised that the monk could speak such perfect English. With a slight reverential stutter, Alex responded, "Indeed, venerable Sir. Could you help us, please? We were hired by the commissioner to find the one that got stolen from here. However, we believe there is a dispute over its authenticity. We were hoping you would be able to shed some light on the matter, please?"

There was an awkward silence in the room as the old man paused flashing another broad smile of glistening gums before finally answering.

"Do not dwell in the past, do not dream of the future, concentrate the mind on the present moment."

As if his answer was to conclude the meeting, he sat back in his chair and folded his hands in his lap. Alex tried to clear the dry spot in her throat. She couldn't help wonder if this was a test of some kind. Not quite knowing how to respond, she cleared her throat and made another attempt.

"Thank you Sir, however, it is imperative we know if indeed there was another urn and more-so, where we might find it. We would really..."

The old man raised his pale hand to stop her from speaking any further.

"There is nothing more dreadful than the habit of doubt. Doubt separates people. It is a poison that disintegrates friendships and breaks up pleasant relations. It is a thorn that irritates and hurts. It is a sword that kills."

Alex felt defeated. Nothing this old man said made any sense.

"Sir, I wholeheartedly agree with your statement, thank you, but could you however be just a tad more precise and direct us to where you think the urn might be?" She was losing her patience. Perhaps her irritation lay with Ollie for leading them on. She wasn't sure. All she knew was that they had flown all this way to South-East Asia and was nowhere nearer to finding the mysterious golden urn.

The monk turned to the side and said something to his caregiver who promptly bowed and left the room. Sam looked at Alex who looked as dazed and confused as he did. She wasn't sure what was going on either but decided to probe even further.

"Venerable Sir, we were hired to retrieve the urn, but in almost a month we are nowhere nearer to finding it. There has to be something you remember that might assist us."

Alex elbowed Ollie, who sat next to her in a silent cry for help. He ignored her, so she nudged harder. It was like elbowing a statue. The man didn't even flinch. She felt her blood boiling with irritation as neither Ollie nor Roshi spoke a word or did anything to help her. It was several minutes of total silence before the old man finally spoke again.

"Patience is key. Remember, a jug fills drop by drop."

Alex bit her lip so hard she was certain she tasted the very drop of blood he just spoke of. This was ridiculous; an utter waste of time, she thought. This man, as wise as he apparently is, will bring them nothing but useless pearls of wisdom. He is nothing but a toothless bag of bones speaking in parables. She was just about to get up and leave when the caregiver returned. Sam, who had sensed her unrest, pulled her down by her arm and watched the young monk walk across the room and hand the old man a rolled up red cloth. Instantly Alex's eyes lit up. Her heart gave several beats, and it took immense effort to stay seated. Sam gave her arm a squeeze. Perhaps this was it. Could it be the original golden urn, or possibly the clue they have been waiting for? Both Alex and Sam's eyes were fixed on the red cloth in the old man's lap. Even Ollie and Roshi straightened up. The painstaking process of watching a hundred-and-two-year-old man unwrap something was worse than watching paint dry. Alex glanced sideways at Sam's clenched hands in his lap. His white knuckles were proof enough that he too needed to restrain himself from jumping up to help. Both Ollie and Roshi, on the other hand, sat calmly with eyes closed. Were they praying for him to finish faster or genuinely as disciplined as they looked?

It felt like an eternity when the last knot was untied to reveal a flat wooden box that was polished to a brilliant luster. The old man looked up and handed Roshi the wooden box who placed it in front of Alex on the floor. Alex could barely contain herself. It wasn't considered sanctimonious for monks to hand anything directly to a female so this she understood. But was she allowed to open it up, she wondered.

"Go on Sheila. You were ready to bolt five minutes ago, yet here you are. Open it up."

Even Ollie's sarcasm bounced like arrows off her back. She couldn't be bothered. The excitement was far too sweeping to be snuffed by anything. She slowly opened the latch and lifted the lid. Inside lay a perfectly preserved scroll tied in place by a yellow ribbon.

"Remember, not getting what you want, is sometimes a wonderful stroke of luck," said the old man.

"Can I read it?" Alex replied in a barely audible voice to which he smiled another toothless smile and nodded.

Her hands were shaking. She had opened up many clues in her young life, but this one seemed to take the cake somehow. Perhaps it was because she sensed danger and secrets around finding an artifact that decidedly had more significance than just being a religious symbol. The knot in the yellow ribbon was tight and required quite a firm tug at it to unravel. Careful to not damage the paper she gently pulled the trimming off and extended the slightly yellowed paper.

"How old is this?" she asked.

"As old as the sun and the stars," the old man replied with yet again another answer with many words but no meaning.

The relic looked at least a hundred years old, but it was in pristine condition. The paper was a pale yellow in color and much thicker and firmer than ordinary white photocopy paper or papyrus. Sam joined in by gently rubbing the sheet between his fingers.

"Remarkable, I've never seen anything like it," he commented.

"That's because it is palm leaf and not paper," Ollie added.

"Yes, Marut, you remember well," the senior monk rendered toward Ollie causing Alex to look at him questioningly before glancing at Sam. She was intrigued now more than ever as to how Ollie knew all this.

"But it looks just like paper," she ventured further to establish just how much this Aussie knew.

His inflated ego led him to fall hook, line, and sinker for it.

"Well, it's quite a craft, Sheila. There were very few who knew this skill. The paper came from the Buong trees that were quite rare in itself and was only found in isolated mountainous areas. The young leaves were cut and dried in the sun before it was cut up into strips. A scribe employed only by the king used a pointed iron tool to carefully carve out each letter and word. Can you imagine the precision and hand control? It's bonkers."

Alex and Sam examined the document with great interest. The carvings under her fingers felt like braille.

"So which king wrote this?" Sam questioned Roshi.

"It is believed to have been king Norodom. He passed it to his brother, king Sisowat who took over his reign in 1903."

"So it is in fact over a century old! That's astounding but what does it say?" Alex asked passing it to Ollie, much to her reluctance.

"No bloody clue, Sheila. None of us know. Those squiggles aren't French, Khmer or Mandarin. It's some sort of a code or something. It's been locked in that box for years. Apparently came with the urn you're after."

"You had better not be messing with me, Ollie," Alex warned only to be interrupted by Rhoshi clearing his throat urging her to keep her voice down. She bowed apologetically and pulled her camera from her bag.

"May I please, Sir?"

Accepting the quick nod in agreement from the elderly monk she snapped several photos of the opened leaf scroll in Ollie's hand.

"If you are facing the right direction, all you need to do is keep walking," the senior monk whispered before looking to Roshi with a nod.

"It's time to go Miss Hunt," Roshi prompted and swiftly tied the scroll and placed it back in its box and wrapped cloth.

"Thank you Great Venerable. It was an honor," Alex bowed in gratitude and turned to follow Roshi and the others back to the foyer.

B arely outside the room, Alex shrieked in elation. "Can you believe it, Sam? How magnificent was that scroll? Not to mention that we met the Great Senior Patriarch of Cambodia! How many archaeologists can record that? Do you know how many would kill to have their hands on this information?"

"You better believe it!" Sam replied. "Have you forgotten someone already tried? We need to keep a tight lid on this, Alex. If word gets out about the scroll's existence, those thugs might just come back for us. We have no idea who they're working for or why they're after us, so we have to be cautious, okay?"

"Okay, Debbie Downer. Deflate my balloon all you want. This was one incredible meeting and I can't wait to flip my laptop open to find out what that scroll says."

"You're welcome, Sheila," a smug Ollie interrupted. "I guess it pays to have me as an ally, doesn't it?"

"Yes, yes okay, you win. Thank you."

"See, now that wasn't so hard was it, Sheila?"

"I wish you would call me Alex, please? Besides, we still need to find out what is written in that scroll. It might be nothing of significance whatsoever, but I have to try."

Ollie exclaimed a loud laugh. "Tell you what, Sheila. If there's nothing of significance in a scroll only about ten people in the entire world ever laid eyes on, then I'll never eat a bear again. Deal?"

"Sounds like a good deal to me," Sam laughed. "On the other hand, Ollie, I would gladly frighten a bear straight into your arms for a plate of your bear stew right now."

The two men's laughter echoed through the monastery's court-yard as they made their way back down to the secret tunnel and through the secret entrance. Once outside in the forest, they bid their farewells to Ollie and Roshi who insisted Ollie had to stay another night. The two men quickly disappeared back through the veil of shrubbery leaving Alex and Sam to find their way back to their motorbike that was still parked under the tree.

"All right then, Alex. There's one positive thing about these monks rising before the sun is up. It's only now time for breakfast where we're heading. What do you say we go hunt down a proper English breakfast and a shower back at the hotel?"

"Thought you'd never ask, Dr. Quinn. I reckon it's exactly what the doctor ordered."

CHAPTER SEVEN
Phnom Penh, Cambodia

Back at the hotel, Alex and Sam freshened up and met up downstairs in the restaurant. As usual, the dining area was filled entirely with exhilarated tourists. It was a bustle of clanging cutlery and irrelevant chatter. Sam, who got to the table first, recognized several British and Australian tourists with a few Dutch patriots scattered in between. Oblivious to the world around him, he tucked into his plate that brimmed with fresh waffles and bacon drenched with maple syrup and bananas.

"Are you feeding an entire army off that plate?" Alex commented as she sat down opposite him.

Sam's mouth was stuffed from cheek to cheek. "You bet! An army of starved cells in my body yes. What you got there?" noticing a brown manila envelope in her hand.

"I had the pictures of the scroll printed at the front desk. There has to be some way of decrypting it. I mean, I get that it was written over a hundred years ago, but someone has to know how to read it, right? I figured we start with Mr. San Yeng-Pho. Perhaps he knows of someone who can help us understand what it says."

Alex reached over and snatched a piece of crispy bacon off his plate. Her laptop was already open as she frantically searched the web for any possible match to the ancient writing. She flipped through website after website, image after image, and nothing.

"There's nothing anywhere. I've traced it back to all the royals who reigned in Cambodia at the time and nothing."

"Try the French archives. Remember, the French tried to take over Southeast Asia and forced the king to comply with French protectorate over Cambodia. Perhaps something similar was communicated between them and somehow found its way to France."

Alex stared in amazement at him over her coffee cup.

"Well, aren't you in top form today? Did you swallow the history books last night?"

Sam chuckled proudly as he stuffed another forkful of food in his mouth.

"I think you're right. We need to try and timestamp the exact period of the scroll's origin. Am I right in remembering Roshi said it was passed from king to king?"

"Hundred percent; I recall him saying it was handed from king Norodom to king Sisowat."

Alex frantically thrashed out some keys on her laptop and then paused with a puzzled look on her face.

"Nope. There's no record of how it came into the hands of king Norodom. He ruled Cambodia from February 1834 to April 1904; seventy years! That's practically his entire life."

Sam dropped his fork and pushed his plate away. "That's it, I can't fit another mouthful in." He reached for the manila envelope and pulled out the printed copy of the scroll to study.

"Is this even writing? It looks like the squiggles we had to learn in kindergarten; a bunch of wave drawings with dots on. From what I can see there aren't any numbers on it either. No dates, names or anything," Sam paused before commenting further as he turned the paper upside down. "What about the actual paper? Can you find any information on the paper? Ollie said it was some kind of palm leaf."

"Good point," Alex responded excitedly before moving her fingers over the keyboard again.

"Okay, here's something. The medium dates back to just over a hundred years old. Definitely, a leaf from the Buong tree, as Ollie said. Before this, they used stone or bamboo planks to write on." She paused briefly and then added, "but that doesn't add up. Norodom was on the throne until 1904 so this substance only came into being after he seized his reign."

"It is entirely possible that the 'over a hundred years' fell within the last years of his reign," Sam added to which Alex nodded in agreement.

"True," tapping away on her keys again.

Moments later a front of house attendant was at their table.

"You have a telephone call, Miss Hunt. Please follow me."

"A telephone call? From who?" but the skinny young woman didn't answer so Alex followed her lead to the front desk where the receiver lay on the counter.

"Hello?"

"Good day Miss Hunt. Please hold for a call from the Commissioner," the female voice announced on the other end of the line.

A cheery Mr. San Yeng-Pho's voice came through the receiver seconds later informing Alex that they had found their stolen vehicle twenty miles north of Oudong. There was no evidence to indicate whom the thieves were and that they had returned it to the rental company.

"That's great news, Mr. San Yeng-Pho, thank you. As it happens, I wanted to run something by you. We found a lead that might help us find the golden urn in question, or at the very least dispel the legend that it wasn't the original one. It is roughly a hundred-year-old sacred document made from Buong leaf and was passed between kings. It may carry some valuable information to aid us in our quest. The only problem is, it is written in a language not known to the lay man on the street. It doesn't appear to be Khmer or Mandarin. Could you by any chance point us to someone who might have the ability to translate the written text, please?"

There was a brief moment of silence on the line before the Commissioner spoke with a tone Alex couldn't quite place. She scrambled for a piece of paper and pen from the front desk and took down the name and address he gave her before returning to their table.

"And? What was that all about?" Sam queried as Alex took her seat.

"It was Mr. San Yeng-Pho. They found the car. He also gave me this name and address in Tri Ton and said this man will be able to help with interpreting the information on the scroll. Apparently dried leaf inscriptions were mainly used to record Khmer prayers and descriptions of historical events so if two kings communicated with it then the information would be encrypted and of great significance. He said that there is a pagoda in another town called Soc Trang which is said to have over a hundred of these Buddhist prayer books preserved. The documents are also known as Sa-tra in the Khmer language."

Sam took the piece of paper.

"Excellent work, Miss Hunt. Then that's where we'll start isn't it?"

Sam pulled the map from his backpack on the floor. "Let's see. Tri Ton, Tri Ton, Tri...got it! It's in the An Giang province that is south from here just inside the Vietnam border. Guess we're going to Vietnam," an elated Sam announced folding the map back into his bag.

"This excites you doesn't it Quinn? It seems the archaeology bug has bitten good and proper," Alex smiled.

"Are you kidding? Something tells me that scroll was far more important than we know for it to come out of the woodworks now. Besides, I'm always up for a little adventure, even if only to keep you out of trouble."

Tri Ton, Vietnam

Forty-five minutes later the two had checked out of their hotel and were in a hired car making the three-and-a-half hour trip to Vietnam. The smooth drive took them past several rice fields laced with workers harvesting the rice. They drove through smaller traditional villages where small groups of excited kids came running up to the car waving and shouting in greeting. Colorful local markets displayed everything from fresh vegetable stalls to bright colored clothing and fabric stands that were crammed with tourists. Outside the villages, lush green scenery prevailed for most of the trip.

It was early evening when they arrived in Tri Ton. The town buzzed with locals on their scooters while bright neon lights lit up the umpteen bars and clubs located on every street and its corner. It was nearly impossible to drive the car through the hoards of commuters rushing home. Deciding it was smarter to leave the car parked and set off on foot, Alex and Sam pulled over on the outskirts of the town and set off toward downtown Tri Ton on foot.

Ladies of the night paraded the curbs looking to earn a living off the libidinous male tourists who window-shopped to their heart's delight. Some 'ladies' looked deceivingly more like men in wigs plastered with make-up and artificial nails while loud American music filled the streets from all angles in an attempt to compete with each other in attracting business. The energetic atmosphere was the exact opposite of what one experienced during the day. It was very much alive and almost electric.

As dusk fell and it became nighttime, the commuters died down and left nothing but crammed bars, flashing lights and scantily clad pole dancers in their wake.

Alex gripped her backpack tighter, and Sam took hold of her hand as added protection. Though crime wasn't prevalent in Vietnam, petty theft was undoubtedly rife. The pair walked the crowded curbs with caution until they found the street Mr. San Yeng-Pho had directed them to.

"I think this is it," Sam said. "Yup, this is the street. I just don't have the foggiest which house it would be. There aren't any numbers anywhere."

The street was located in downtown Tri Ton, and there wasn't a tourist in sight. Instead, locals overcrowded the curbs outside overly seedy looking bars filled with half naked woman serving drinks at the tables. Heavily tattooed men were laden with gold chains, and clouds of cigarette smoke lay thick in the air. Above the bars were dingy looking apartments decorated with laundry hanging from just about every window balcony. Suspicious stares greeted them as they passed the exposed bars.

Sam gripped Alex's hand tighter and moved his other hand over his tummy where he had secured his revolver under his shirt in his jean's waistband. Being out at night amongst the tourists in the uptown streets was relatively safe, but being out here, required a different kind of courage.

"I think we should turn back, Sam," Alex whispered.

"I agree, let's walk up that street over there."

They had trailed off down the road too far to turn around. The end of the street was in sight. Alex glanced sideways into one of the nightclubs where a grubby looking Asian man was halfway through his addiction at a small table that stood in plain sight. On his one knee was a topless prostitute cheering him on while, hanging over his shoulders, another one was pulling the rubber band tighter around his arm. He looked up and winked at Alex, sending uncomfortable quivers down her spine. Nervous tremors paralyzed her legs which slowed her pace as she tried to keep up with Sam whom forcefully pushed their way through a drunken crowd in front of them. Suddenly Sam stopped and she slammed into him from behind.

"Why are you stopping Sam? Let's get out of here!"

Sam didn't answer. Instead, he hurriedly changed direction and pulled her across the street. The scene on the other side of the road was much the same; lined with seedy bars and clubs. Sam's pace quickened. His attention seemed to be pinned to something up ahead.

"Sam, what's wrong?" Alex urged.

"We're being followed," he answered abruptly. "Pick up the pace, Alex."

A flustered Alex turned to see who he was referring to and spotted two Asian men behind her and two more on the opposite pavement. They bore a striking similarity to the thugs on the motorbikes.

"It's the same guys that were on the bikes, Sam!"

Sam didn't answer. He knew that already. They pushed through the crowd bumping several drunken locals who shouted in anger after them. Sam scoured the area in search of an escape route but every street he looked up was as sleazy as the one they were already in. He spotted an alleyway up ahead and glanced to his left to eyeball the stalkers. Alex kept her eyes on the ones behind them. They had already gained ground. If they kept heading straight the thugs would impede them up ahead. If they turn back, they'd run into the ones behind them. Apart from the dark side alley they were trapped. It was their only option and by this time both Alex and Sam were in a light jog as they raced to get to the alley before the thugs got there. They had no idea where the narrow passageway would lead them, but it was their only chance of escaping them alive.

Sam picked up the pace. His long strides jerked Alex into a run to keep up. The group of men picked up speed too and started closing in on them. Sam tightened his grip on Alex's hand who by now was a dangling mess behind Sam as she tried to keep up. She gripped the cord of her backpack over her shoulder to stop it from hitting against her back and throwing her off momentum. They got to the alley first. A good sixty-five feet ahead of their pursuers. The alley was deserted, dark and reeked of danger. Sam pulled Alex closer to his side.

"Run, Alex! We need to gain ground!" He let go of her hand affording her a far more comfortable running stance. Their feet hit the poorly paved road with a thunderous thumping that echoed off the walls on either side of the narrow passage. There wasn't a human in sight anywhere and even if there were, they'd no doubt be as dangerous as these thugs. The buildings on either side had several wooden doors and windows that were shut tight. It was dangerously dark and eerie. They kept running, as fast as they could. Alex looked back and saw the men turning up into the alley behind them.

"Sam, they're right behind us! What do we do?"

Sam looked back. The guys were easily a hundred feet behind them concluding they had a slight advantage over them.

"We keep running, Alex! As fast as our feet can take us! Don't look back! Just RUN!"

On cue, Alex propelled forward into a sprint keeping her eyes on the neon lights at the end of the alley which was at least another three-hundred feet ahead. The men's feet thumped on the tar road behind them but Alex forced herself not to turn and look back at them. She needed to remain focussed. If they're in luck, the street up ahead should be the main street separating the tourist neighborhood from downtown. Directly in front of them was a just-below-the-hip high barrier closing off the alleyway to the main road. They would have to attempt to jump over it. There's no time to stop now. Alex silently shot up a prayer that her five foot seven body would make the jump. Fear gripped her throat as she came closer to the railing. She had no choice. Thirty feet or so on the other side of that obstruction they'd reach safety. As if Sam sensed her fear, he yelled out, "You can do this, Alex! One high jump that's all!"

Her breathing was unstable and her lungs burned under the strain of her full sprint as she came closer to the barrier. Panic strangled her throat as she tried to figure out which leg to extend in front of her. Adrenaline soared through her veins as she leaped over the railing but seconds later her chin hit the asphalt and she felt the burning pain in her knees and hands as the gravel ripped through her flesh. In a panic she looked back at the men who were fast gaining on them. She felt Sam's strong hands in her armpits as he pulled her up from the ground and threw her over his shoulder. She wasn't quite sure what hurt more; her bleeding wounds or Sam's shoulder pushing into her tummy as he ran toward the lights. Facing down she had no way of seeing how far they were from the main road but what she could see when she lifted her head was one of the men pointing his gun directly behind them.

"Gun! Sam, they're going to shoot!"

Sam panted heavily, unable to speak under the extreme burden of carrying Alex while in a full sprint. Alex tried to reach for Sam's gun that was tucked under his shirt in front of his pants but couldn't. A bullet whooshed by them quickly followed by a succession of open fire. Sam ducked and ran for cover at the side of the road. The neon lights were right in front of them. He needed to be on the opposite side of the road to turn up around the corner to get to their car. Shots resounded above the nearing club music as the bullets whistled through his feet and legs. He couldn't go any faster. Though Alex was small-framed and feather lite, his feet couldn't gather any more speed. His thighs were on fire as his muscles took strain under the run. They were out of options. He had to risk the firing bullets and cross the street to get them to safety. He swerved to the left, almost throwing Alex off his shoulder. She groaned as his shoulder pushed harder into her belly leaving her gasping for air. The bullets stopped just as they turned the corner onto the pavement and rammed through a group of festive tourists who soon after, realized what they had been running from.

Frazzled screams echoed in the night air as a number of people were shoved out of the way.

Alex and Sam crossed the busy street in a final attempt to disappear amongst the crowd. Their car was just ahead. He had to keep going until they were safe. Stopping now wasn't an option. Alex lifted her head and surveyed the entrance to the alleyway behind them that now lay bare in their wake. They had lost them. The thugs were nowhere in sight.

"I think they're gone, Sam. You can put me down now. I think I can walk."

Sam ignored her. He wasn't sprinting anymore, but he wasn't slowing down either. Alex looked sideways and recognized the bar that was opposite their parked car. There was no mistaking it since the particular venue took up substantial space and was open to the road, clearly recognizable by the enormous tiger-head ornaments that decorated the sides of the building with a dozen more smaller ones hanging over the elongated bar counter. The lights were a brilliant white, illuminating most of the street which was why they had parked the car there in the first place, thinking it would be safest under the bright lights.

Alex's calves hit the hard metal of the car before she propelled backward onto the hood. Sam circled the car and yanked open the back door before coming back around to pick her up. It all happened so fast. Before she could object, she was thrown into the backseat with Sam jumping behind the wheel and speeding off. He hadn't said a word and was gasping for air. His foot slammed down on the accelerator, clearly still governed by adrenaline.

"We lost them, Sam, it's okay," Alex said with a broken voice as the tears pooled in her eyes.

Sam looked in the rearview mirror and caught sight of Alex's consoling eyes. He slowed the car down. Blood gushed from her chin and had trickled down her neck.

"We lost them, Sam," she repeated. His eyes were the size of saucers; evidence that he was still in shock.

"Are you okay?" he asked speaking for the first time since the chase started.

Alex nodded. "You?"

Sam wasn't sure. He patted his chest and arms and stopped as his hand felt the saturated patch on the side of his thigh. A pool of blood lay on the seat under his leg.

Noticing something was amiss Alex sat up and leaned forward.

"You're shot! Sam they shot you!"

Alex frantically climbed between the seats and sat down in the passenger seat to get a better glimpse of his leg.

"Sam stop, you need to pull over. There's a lot of blood."

Sam's face had already turned a pale white.

"Don't you pass out on me, Sam Quinn, do you hear me? Pull over!"

He did as she instructed and pulled over in a nearby no parking zone, scraping the front wheel against the curb.

Alex jumped out and hobbled around the car. She yanked open the driver's door and noticed the extent of Sam's wound for the first time. It was bad, very bad. His jeans were drenched in blood. Sam was quiet. She pulled her belt from her pants and tied it just above the wound to stop the bleeding. She bent down and drew her pocketknife from her boot and sliced through the wet fabric, ripping it open to expose the gaping gunshot wound.

Alex fought to hide the shock on her face, drawing back a quick breath as she looked down at the exposed flesh and fast-flowing blood. "Sam, this is bad. It's really bad. We need to get you to the hospital."

"No," Sam groaned. "They'll find us there. You're going to need to remove the bullet yourself. Get us to a hotel."

"You're insane! Have you lost your marbles, Quinn? I'm not a doctor! No way!"

Sam gripped her hand and pinned her eyes with his. "You can do this Alex. I won't be able to do it myself. I'd need a steady hand so I don't puncture an artery. Besides there's a good chance I will lose consciousness from the pain. I'll guide you through it as far as I can but we'd need to go now before I lose any more blood."

CHAPTER EIGHT

Alex couldn't breathe. Her mouth was dry and her heart was still beating in her throat. When the adrenaline wore off the panic suddenly took over but she couldn't allow herself to lose control now. Sam needed her, for once, he needed *her*! She looked at his face as his head lay back against the seat's headrest. He wasn't looking well at all. His face was deathly pale, and he was losing a lot of blood. She grabbed her backpack from the backseat and pulled out her headscarf. Sam groaned each time she tightened it around the wound. She had no idea where she learned to do this, but it seemed to help somehow. She stood up and frantically looked around for a place to take up shelter. She's going to have to find a smaller hotel so she could sneak him past the front desk unnoticed, but where? She had no idea where they were.

"Okay, think, Alex," she said out loud to herself. Seconds later she ducked back down into the car and tugged Sam's arm. He was already in a semi-conscious state.

"Sam!" She patted him against his cheek. "Sam stay with me. I need to get you into the backseat so I can drive."

She tugged on his arm again, but it had minimal effect. He was barely lucid and too tall and heavy for her to manage. She pulled at his other arm and slapped him gently across his cheek in an effort to wake him up.

"Sam wake up, you can't sleep now. I need to move you."

Sam opened his eyes and she wrapped his one arm around her neck and over her shoulders. His body was heavy on her tiny frame even with him doing most of the standing now on his own.

"That's it, steady now."

With great effort, she finally managed to get him into the back-seat and propped his wounded leg on top of her backpack before settling in behind the steering wheel. The pool of blood on the black leather seat made a gushing sound as she sat down behind the wheel of the car and she felt the still warm liquid instantly penetrate her pants, drenching it within seconds. There was no time to clean up now. She had to get him to a hotel. It was dark outside and there were very few buildings or lights where they were parked next to the side of the road. Seat-belt on and engine running she caught sight of the stick shift. Her heart sank in her shoes. She hadn't ever driven anything other than an automatic car. The figure H on the knob gave her some guideline but getting it to move into first gear proved somewhat challenging.

She apologized out loud as the gear made a screeching noise while she frantically tried to get it into the right gear. A couple of attempts later she got it and slipped the car off the pavement and back onto the road causing Sam's leg to bounce off the back-pack. He let out a despairing groan as the pain shot through his wound.

"Oops!" She offered apologetically glancing at him in her mirror. His face told her exactly how much pain he was in. Once again he was barely lucid now and he settled his head back against the seat and closed his eyes. Tiny beads of sweat trickled into his hairline. She would have to get cracking, before it's too late.

The road was relatively quiet as they drove away from the village. It wasn't a big village to begin with and apart from a few hotels, there weren't that many options to choose from. She would first need to find supplies to clean out the wound though, she thought. Removing a bullet requires more than just a towel and water. Her stomach turned as she realized she had no idea what supplies she would need. She could hardly ask the pharmacist for advice on how to remove a bullet. Her eyes searched frantically on both sides of the dark street. There had to be a shopping mart of some kind open somewhere, Alex thought. The buildings on either side of the road started to become less frequent and Alex realized she was probably too far out of town. She'd have to go back toward the clubs. The car screeched again as she dropped a gear to turn the car around and head back down the street toward the village. A small distance further, she turned another corner and went down a road with a couple more rowdy bars and flashing lights when she spotted a barely visible shop tucked between a closed gas station and a cheap clothing boutique. The neon yellow 'OPEN' sign in the window flickered on and off. Elated that it appeared they might be open she stopped to have a closer look. The lights were on inside but there was no movement. She decided to at least try so she pulled the car over next to the curb.

"Stay still, Sam. Be back in a jiffy."

Sam didn't react. He was deathly pale and barely conscious. She jumped out and ran up to the door. The soft chimes of a bell startled her as she pushed the door open. A young Asian woman behind the counter briefly looked up from her mobile phone and nodded. Then looked at Alex's bloodstained pants and pointed to the back of the shop.

The shop was long and narrow with rows of tightly packed products ranging from essential consumables to pet food. Alex lowered her head and hurried between the confined shelves to the back of the shop where there was a small dispensary section. Her heart skipped a beat as she noticed the assistant's eyes on her bloodstained pants. She scoured the shelves for anything that might be of use. A couple glass bottles of clear liquid stared back at her. The labels were written in Mandarin, but she recognized the word for alcohol in the content list. She had no clue what the rest of the words on the bottle meant. She bit her thumbnail and then decided to take the one with a picture that resembled a plaster. A pack of bandages lay on the shelf next to the bottles of which she grabbed two and then snatched a packet of five sterilizing cloths off the shelf next to it. She bent down and moved her eyes rapidly over several baskets on the bottom shelf that was filled with all sorts of paraphernalia. She was looking for a pair of tweezers or small pliers she might need to pull the bullet out with. She startled when the shop assistant suddenly appeared next to her and handed her a shopping basket before taking her place again behind the counter. The basket contained a bottle of whiskey, several rolls of cotton swabs, the pliers she was looking for along with a new pair of pants and some painkillers. Alex wasn't sure if she felt embarrassment for getting caught or joy that she got help. Either way, she headed to the cashier with a bashful smile. The woman merely nodded, popped it into a brown paper bag, and slid it across the counter. Alex nodded back self-consciously. It didn't take a rocket scientist to figure out that this woman had done this before. That was very obvious. Without a further word exchanged between them, Alex paid and picked the bag up from the counter. The woman's hand slammed down on the bag sending trembles of fear down Alex's spine. She looked up at her in horror. Did she want money in exchange for her silence? Alex took out a couple more notes from her pocket, but the woman ignored it. Instead, she reached under the counter and pulled out a business card then popped it into the shopping bag and handed it back to Alex. Stunned Alex grabbed the bag, threw her a smile and, with trembling legs, hurried back to the car.

In the safety of the car, she locked the doors and looked back at Sam whose condition was still unchanged. The road was too quiet for her liking. The place gave her the creeps.

"Hang on Sam. I have everything we need. At least, I think I do."

She pulled the business card from the shopping bag and read the name of a motel and address. Could she trust this woman? She had no choice. She popped the address into the GPS, screeched the gears into place again and sped off.

Five minutes later they pulled up next to a derelict motel in the middle of nowhere. The signage out front hung by a single black wire while all the other lights were off. There was no sign of any life. The unpretentious parking lot in the front was an empty patch of sand, but she pulled into it nevertheless. She switched the car off and suspiciously stared at the quiet building. It was in a serious state of disrepair and backed up against a forest of tall trees and dense shrubs. From the front it had a single blue front door and windows on either side. It was extremely basic and certainly didn't look anything like a motel of any kind. Built entirely from half rotten wooden planks, it rather resembled an old run down shack in the middle of the forest than a motel. She looked at the business card again and checked the GPS. It was indeed the right place. As if to prompt her to get on with it, Sam whimpered soft moans from the backseat. She would have to risk it. The woman from the shop had been quite agreeable and very helpful so she had no reason to doubt that she was perhaps leading her into a trap.

Alex got out of the car, skimming into the darkness once more while walking up to the entrance. It was deathly silent. A soft breeze cut through the lush trees behind the house. She opened the door to find an empty reception in a poorly lit room. On the counter was a money box with a sign simply showing KHR20 000. Converted, twenty-thousand Cambodian Riel was a little over twenty pounds. She slipped the amount into the box, grabbed a room key from the orange shoebox next to it and dashed back out to the car.

"Sam, wake up. I found a place to stay the night."

Sam whimpered softly as she pulled him up from the backseat of the car and propped her body under his armpit. Her back-pack and bag with medicinal supplies hung over her other shoulder. Thankfully there were no stairs. Tiny droplets of blood left a trail in the sand from the car to the front door as they slowly entered the motel and made their way to their room down the passage. Sam was lucid enough to limp through the door and hastily flopped down on the only double bed in the center of the room. The room was dark and dingy looking but it would suffice. To the right was a small bathroom from which Alex quickly grabbed a couple of threadbare towels and positioned it under Sam's injured leg before rummaging through the drawers in the room. In the closet opposite the bed was a padded cotton sheet similar to the ones used in the hospitals, which Alex thought very odd, but nevertheless quickly used to replace the bathroom towels with. A small stainless steel kettle stood on the desk under the window along with a tall silver cup, a matching flat dish and a small pair of sharp scissors. This was no ordinary motel, that's certain. She popped the kettle on and hurried to the bathroom to clean her hands. Light pink water ran into the small white basin as the water washed off Sam's blood. She looked up into the mirror above the basin. She felt like vomiting. *What in heaven's name have they gotten themselves into?* She thought, and splashed cold water over her face. "Right, let's do this," she said to herself in the mirror before heading back out to pour hot water from the kettle into the flat silver dish. Her knife clanked against the metal as she dropped it into the hot water to sterilize it. Minutes later she had the items of the shopping bag spread out on the bed. Now what? Hands on her hips she stared down at the contents unsure where to start. From the corner of her eye, her once bright patterned scarf around Sam's thigh was drenched in blood. She looked back at the dispensary on the bed next to him and grabbed the bottle of whiskey and took several gulps from the bottle. The bitter liquid burned her throat but she took two more big gulps before lifting Sam's head and putting the bottle to his lips. He took several swigs and dropped his head back onto his pillow. Alex paused and took another large sip before placing the bottle on the nightstand.

The knot in the scarf was too tight, and her fumbling fingers didn't help to get it undone either. She grabbed the scissors and carefully cut through the thin fabric. Alex exhaled in relief as she opened the wound to see that the blood had somewhat stopped. She released her belt that was still tied around his thigh, and cut through the thick denim leg of the pants. A gaping round bullet hole stared back at her. Her stomach churned as the nausea pushed up into her throat. Pausing for just a second to pull herself together again, she lifted Sam's leg to see if by some miracle the bullet might have passed through his leg, but it didn't. There was no exit wound. Her heart sank to the pit of her stomach. There was no way out of it. She'd have to remove this bullet and fast.

"This might hurt a little, Sam. You might want to brace yourself."

Sam needed no warning. His hand reached for the whiskey bottle next to him.

"Yeah, good idea," Alex said as she helped him take several more swigs before taking another one herself.

"I need you sober for this," Sam mumbled while fumbling with his belt buckle in an attempt to remove it himself.

Alex, slightly puzzled, lifted his T-shirt and removed the revolver that was still tucked in his waistband before pulling his belt off.

"Now's not the time and place for this you know," Sam joked subdued.

"Oh stop," she responded shyly and handed him his belt.

Sam bit down hard on the leather strap.

"Okay, ready?"

Sam nodded but his eyes said something entirely different. Alex picked up the steaming hot knife and paused over the gaping hole.

"Are you sure about this, Sam? What if I slice through an artery or something?"

Sam nodded and shut his eyes, biting down harder on the leather strap. The hot blade sliced through his flesh as easily as a hot knife through butter. Much to Alex's surprise, Sam didn't flinch. She proceeded to make a small incision across the hole. Instantly the blood started gushing out. She cursed under her breath as she fought the urge to hurl all over the tacky brown carpet.

She threw the knife back into the hot water and grabbed the bottle of sterilizing liquid. The lid spun off in one rapid twist and fell to the floor. Without hesitation she poured a substantial amount over the wound. Sam squealed with pain as the liquid hit his open wound.

Alex jerked her hand back and cringed in empathy. "Sorry!"

But it seemed to have done the trick. The bleeding stopped. The worst, however, was still to come. She wiped her brow on her sleeve as she readied her fingers over the gaping wound. She couldn't bring herself to look at Sam for fear of seeing his pain and quitting the procedure halfway through. She drew in a deep breath and stuck two fingers into the wound. It was a disgusting feeling. She had imagined it would feel like stuffing garlic cloves into a leg of lamb, but it wasn't. It was hot and sticky instead. Sam groaned as she prodded and probed into his wound. Less than ten seconds later she felt the hard metal object under her forefinger. It was stuck underneath his thigh muscle but luckily hadn't penetrated any bone or fractured it. She reached across Sam and picked up the pliers from the bed with her other hand. It wouldn't reach at that angle, she thought. The dark red blood bubbled up between her fingers. Even with the incision, the hole didn't provide enough space for two of her fingers and the pliers. It wouldn't work. She would have to use her fingers. She couldn't see beyond the pooling blood either so she threw the pliers back down onto the bed. This would be where the surgeon would call for suction, she reflected. Sam moaned in pain again as her fingers started moving around the bullet. She tried not to pay attention to his groans. She had to remain focused. If she did this right it would all be over soon.

She squeezed her fingers together and trapped the bullet between her forefinger and middle finger and slowly pulled her hand out. The clanging noise of the bullet hitting the bottom of the stainless steel cup was music to their ears.

"Ha! I did it! Sam, I did it!" she exclaimed in joy still staring at the giant copper bullet in the bottom of the cup.

Sam's moans had stopped. She looked at him and realized he had passed out. Her eye caught sight of the gaping wound. Blood gushed out like a bubbling fountain. Panic hit her and she grabbed the sterilizing liquid off the nightstand and poured a generous amount into the wound. She pushed the cloth down hard onto the wound. The pressure seemed to help; or possibly the liquid. She wasn't sure and it didn't matter. The bleeding had stopped. All that was left was for her to close the wound somehow. Blast! She hadn't thought that far ahead. Sam had lost a lot of blood so it was crucial. She took his belt that was still clenched between his teeth and tied it tightly around the pressure bandage before removing her belt that was still tied above the wound. It should cancel each other out. In theory, that is. She needed a needle and a thread. She ran across the room to the bathroom and frantically searched the small basket with the complimentary soaps and shampoos. Got it. Her bloodied fingers ripped open the little sewing kit to reveal a rainbow of colored thread and a couple of needles. Back at Sam's side, she yanked a piece of yarn out and pushed it through the needle's eye. Her fingers were sticky from the blood. The thought of sewing through flesh disgusted her, but she had come this far already. It couldn't possibly be more stomach churning than sticking your fingers into a gaping wound. At least Sam wasn't aware of anything now.

The needle pierced through his tough skin forcing her to push down harder on the needle to penetrate the skin. In her mind she was back in Tanzania sitting next to Jelani and her mother, sewing blankets from the animal skins.

Seven stitches later and the wound was closed up; albeit not that neat, it did the trick. She was no seamstress after all.

Another five minutes later and the wound was neatly cleaned and bandaged. She knelt next to the bed and admired her work. She did it. Remarkably, she did it. Tears of relief rolled down her cheeks as a wave of emotion washed over her exhausted body.

In the small bathroom mirror, the sight of her bloodstained hands left streaks across her teary face and her chin and palms had several open scratches from her fall over the railing. She popped into the shower and watched rivers of pink water eventually run clear into the drain trap. The warm, soothing water of the shower was relaxing. She didn't allow her thoughts to trail to tomorrow just yet. What mattered most was that Sam would be fine. Tonight, they both needed their rest.

O n the bed Sam's breathing was stable, and he was still asleep. The bandage was still clean which meant the wound was also in a stable condition. She took a damp towel and gently wiped Sam's face before lying down next to him on the bed. This was not how this relic hunt was supposed to go. Earlier that week she had almost lost her life at the waterfall, and today, Sam nearly lost his. What was it about this urn that stirred up such fuss? She leaned over and grabbed Sam's gun off the side table and tucked it under her pillow. They would have to be alert from here on out and watch their backs. Someone out there is after the precious artifact themselves or, will do whatever it takes for it to stay buried forever no matter the cost, even if it were someone's life. Whatever the reason, it's a relic, and she was hired to find it. Giving up wasn't an option. Discovering the scroll shook things up. It was a dangerous mission, but one they would have to embark on if the truth were ever to be revealed.

CHAPTER NINE

Alex woke at the crack of dawn. Beside her, on the bed, Sam was still sound asleep. She placed her hand on his forehead. There was no sign of a fever and even in the dim light of the room, she could see his coloring had returned to almost normal. That was positive. She walked across to the window and peered through the faded brown curtains. The view was nothing spectacular. Their room looked out onto the forest behind the house. Peering through the tall trees, the sun's rays still sat low. She walked over to the door and popped her head out into the corridor. It was as quiet and desolate as it was the night before. She shut the door again. Sam would be hungry when he woke but she doubted there would be a buffet set up in a dining room somewhere. She would have to leave to find them something to eat and drink. She slipped her shoes on and grabbed her backpack from the chair in the corner and, with her hand on the doorknob, stopped. She should take the gun. Just in case. Sam would be fine until she got back.

With the gun safely tucked in the small of her back, she walked down the quiet corridor toward the reception, expecting to see someone behind the counter. There was still no one. The money box and keys were untouched. The small office behind the desk was also empty. Unsurprisingly there were no other rooms or a dining area where breakfast was served nor another human in sight. Outside the front door, their rental car was still the only one in the barren parking lot. She wiped her brow. It was already hot and humid even though the sun hadn't risen yet.

At her feet, a visible line of blood ran through the sand and stopped at the car so, without hesitation, she quickly dragged her feet across the trail, sweeping the sand over the blood to cover it up. The blood on the car seat had dried entirely during the night, but the mat under the pedals was still soaked. She paused, briefly surveying the area before quickly dumping the soaked mat in the trunk and then casually slipped in behind the wheel. The screeching stick shift echoed loudly through the quiet morning air.

"Oh, stupid thing, come on!" She moaned at it in annoyance as she often got when she had no sleep.

Another couple of tries and she successfully drove off onto the tarred road toward the village. She hadn't realized they were so far out of the town; it was a solid fifteen minutes before dozens of commuters on their mopeds and tuk-tuks raced past her. The small village was already a flurry of chaos as the locals made their way to their workplaces. Leaning forward over the steering wheel, she drove slowly along the bustling road, inviting quite a couple of beeping motorists' horns urging her to get out of their way. Though there were many stalls and supermarkets toward the center of the town, she concluded it would be safest to go back to the shop she had bought the medical supplies from the night before. If she recalled correctly it should be right around the next corner. It wasn't long before she found it. Unlike the night before, there were crates of fresh fruit and vegetables displayed on the sidewalk in front of the door. She slipped the car into the vacant parking a short distance from the shop. Perhaps it was best to hide the car in plain sight she concluded.

The familiar chime of the doorbell announced her presence. To her surprise, the shop assistant from the night before was not there. In her stead was a much older male Alex estimated to be in his retirement years. Perhaps it was her father and the thought crossed her mind if he had any idea of his daughter's associations with protecting citizens.

A young couple stood in the corner deliberating over cold drinks in the fridge in front of them, but apart from them, the shop was empty. Alex moved across to the fridge next to the couple and grabbed two orange juices from the rack and then moved further down the narrow aisle to the opposite end. The shelf displayed an array of quick cook noodles. It will have to do, she thought. She grabbed four containers and carried it close against her chest held in place by her forearm to the checkout. On the counter, a delicious aroma of freshly baked rolls in a basket filled the air, and she popped four into the brown paper bag that lay on the counter next to it. Satisfied with her breakfast selection, she left the shop and was back in the car heading toward their safehouse.

Until now she hadn't been hungry at all but the delicious scent of the fresh bread surged hunger pangs through her body. She reached over to the paper bag on the seat next to her and pulled out one of the rolls. Seconds later the bread roll went flying through the air as a hard knock hit the car from behind, thrusting her head forward.

"What on earth?" She shouted at the black van visible in her rearview mirror. "Watch where you're going!" She shouted throwing her arms in the air.

But it was no accident. Her words had barely been spoken and the van rammed her again. Alex gripped the steering wheel and straightened into the seat. Her eyes were fixed on the rearview mirror as she stared at the two Asian men in the van behind her. Her foot pushed down harder on the accelerator, propelling her car forward. The road lay long and straight ahead of her. Several cars passed her from the front going toward the village. She would reach the safehouse in about ten minutes if she continued. Even so, she can't go there now with them following her. It would expose their hiding place and Sam was in no condition to run on foot anywhere. She watched as the black van gained on her and rammed into her again. This time hard enough to have her lose control of the car and swerve into the oncoming traffic, missing it by a margin before turning back into her lane.

"You're going to kill me!" she shouted as if the Asian men could hear. With the road up ahead clear from any oncoming cars the van gained speed and pulled up next to her. She gathered more speed in a futile attempt to outdrive them, but the minibus followed suit and rammed into her side. Her wheels slipped off the road and hit the gravel, grazing several low bearing shrubs in its path. Fear ripped through her body sending her pulse into a thudding irregular rhythm. She jerked the steering wheel and slammed on the brakes. The vehicle spun around twice and somehow landed back on the road facing the direction of the village.

In her rearview mirror, the black van slammed on its brakes to turn around. This was her chance to get away. Miraculously she shoved the gear into place and sped off toward the village, keeping her eyes pinned on the van that was still trying to make a u-turn behind her. Her heart was beating out of control. Adrenaline soared through her veins as she pushed her foot flat on the accelerator to gain enough distance between them. It didn't take her long to reach the village, and she turned down the now familiar street where her little supply shop was. The street was busy and forced her to slow down. The van was still not in sight. She recalled seeing another road turn up ahead but directly in front of her an elderly lady on her sidecar motorcycle took her sweet time.

"Oh come on lady, move out the way!" she shouted sounding her horn to hurry her along.

The commuter was undeterred by Alex's rudeness behind her and arrogantly stuck to her speed and lane. Alex jerked the car to the left and crossed lanes to overtake the woman, cutting her off as she came back into the right lane. Behind her the black van just turned into the road, crisscrossing past several cars in an attempt to gain on her.

The thought of being caught didn't enter her mind as she fought through the heavy traffic. Alex pushed down on the pedal and almost hit another motorcycle family. She swerved onto the pavement to avoid the family, and collided with several hawkers' trolleys. Colorful umbrellas and fruit pieces exploded into the air.

"Sorry!" She yelled apologetically out the window as she struggled to gain control of the car and bring it back onto the road again. Her eyes spotted the van battling through the busy road behind her. Deciding not to play by the traffic rules anymore, she yanked the wheel directing the car across the opposite lane and turned into a side road, narrowly missing an oncoming vehicle. She had already upset most of the villagers so why stop now? She made another quick turn into a smaller obscured side street and pushed the car to go faster. If her orientation was correct, she was driving back in the direction of the road to the safehouse and parallel to the one they came racing down. The van was nowhere in sight. With any luck she outwitted them. She flung her head around to have a proper look behind her and spotted the nose of the van turning into the road behind her.

Determined to get away she clenched down on her jaw and fixed her gaze on the road ahead. She had no idea how they had managed to track her location but she wasn't about to give up without a fight even if they did have the advantage in knowing these streets back to front. She'd just have to be smart about.

Her eyes scoured both sides of the road, but there was no way out. Apart from a couple of narrow alleyways there were no alternate routes to deviate to. Her foot flattened the accelerator as she sped the car through the thankfully quiet street. The road to the motel was directly ahead, but she still couldn't risk leading them straight to their location. She would circle around again! Yes, that should work.

With a clear plan in her head, she turned left around the block and raced down the busy street. This time, she stopped at nothing and no one. They would have to get out of her way if they didn't want to get run down. By her calculations, the van should have turned into the top road only now. Her eyes frantically scanned for another alley or side road. *There!* She somehow missed it on the first run. Again she swerved the car across the busy road and drove straight into the almost invisible side street that turned out to be an extremely narrow alleyway. The car's nose scraped the brick wall before bouncing off and hitting the opposite wall, taking the side mirror with it. With any luck there would be no way the much larger van would fit between those walls. She hurried the vehicle up the alley which joined up with the parallel street. This shortcut would have shaved off a substantial amount of time and allowed for her to gain a significant distance. If she could just avoid them seeing her altogether and turn the corner in time before they drove down the road behind her she'd be scot-free. She dropped a gear and pushed the pedal hard into the floorboard sending her bouncing into the air when she hit a small bump in the road. Fifty feet...thirty...ten, she turned left into the side street while looking back to see if she beat the van. She did. They must still be stuck in the busy street, she thought with glee. The tires screeched around the corner and her wheels scraped the side-walk, but she had made it. Just ahead lay the road to the motel where she could gain even more distance if she kept her foot on the accelerator. Convinced she was in the clear she decided to risk it. She would turn right onto the road and race like mad for the motel. *It's now or never.*

But every so often her eyes looked up at the rearview mirror. The street was still clear behind her. The road was coming up ahead and the car was traveling at a rapid speed. She would have to hold her pace for her escape to work and hope and pray she doesn't crash into any crossing traffic. She couldn't slow down now much less stop to comfortably make the turn into the street. It was a tight corner and she ran the risk of flipping the car, but it was a risk she was prepared to take.

With her foot flat on the pedal and both hands gripped firmly around the steering wheel, she shut one eye and turned right into the road. The shrill shriek of the wheels against the asphalt road pierced the air as she came around the corner. She felt her body tilt to the side as two of the wheels lifted off the road. An oncoming tuk-tuk just escaped the rear of the car and she swung the steering into the opposite direction, thumping the two airborne wheels back down on the ground. She could no longer feel her heart that five minutes ago still hammered hard against her chest. Her legs were too numb to release her foot from the floor pedal and she barely blinked. It was a race against time now so she kept going never once looking back.

She had no idea how she had managed to get to the motel parking in one piece, but she did. That was all that mattered. Afraid the van would undoubtedly spot her car in the parking, she drove around the back of the building in between the tall trees and parked the vehicle practically right outside their bedroom window. The car was entirely concealed and would not be visible from the road.

It was only when she switched the ignition off that she was conscious of breathing again and she lifted her hands that were shaking uncontrollably off the wheel. She flung the door open, desperate to get some air, and fell to the ground. Her lungs drew in gasps of oxygen as she struggled to maintain control over her body. Sam! She had been gone for hours and never left him a note. He would be worried sick by now, or dead. She pulled her body up against the car, making every effort to calm her rattling knees. The bag of breakfast supplies on the passenger seat had fallen off onto the floor and she felt the hard edge of the driver's seat push through her tummy as she stretched across to the passenger side to shove the noodles and scattered bread rolls back into the bag. With the shopping bag and her backpack in hand she pushed the motel's door open. She was a rattling mess when she burst into their hotel room and slammed the door behind her.

The commotion startled Sam who had been sitting up in bed waiting for her. On impulse, he instinctively grabbed the metal dish from the side table and flung it at the door. Alex ducked and just missed the metal object from hitting her arm.

"What the... Alex, you scared the daylights out of me! I could have killed you!" Sam let out.

"Not likely, you throw like a girl," she said trying hard to hide her still trembling body.

She should have known she couldn't hide anything from Sam. His startled look instantly turned to concern.

"What's wrong? Are you ok? Where have you been?" Sam fired questions at her.

Alex walked over to the bathroom and splashed several hands full of cold water on her face. Sam knew something bad had happened when she returned, her hands still shaking. He gently squeezed her hand and pulled her down to sit next to him on the bed.

"Alex, talk to me. This is me, remember? You know you don't have to raise your guard with me."

Sam was right. Alex trusted him with her life. He always made her feel safe.

She lifted her head and allowed the tears to run freely down her cheeks.

"They almost got me, Sam. They almost got me," she sobbed uncontrollably.

Sam pulled her head to his chest and held her tight.

"Shh, you're safe now, calm down. It's okay."

Alex raised her head, wiped her face, and stared into his eyes. "How is it that you're always so strong, Sam? I am supposed to give you TLC for a change. You're the patient remember?" She said with a faint smile.

Sam cupped her face with his hand. "Right now, I think, you might need it more than me."

His hand felt strong and tender on her skin, and she found herself leaning into his hand for added comfort. Unfamiliar feelings warmed her insides where moments ago it was still gripped by fear. She knew she felt safe with Sam, but this? This she couldn't quite explain. She jumped to her feet quickly and wiped her face with her sleeve before moving to the door to pick up the shopping bag from the floor.

"I got breakfast. It's not waffles and bacon, but it will have to do." She pulled out the containers of quick cooking noodles. "I also have fresh orange juice," she added with a smile, avoiding his eyes.

Within minutes she had busied herself with boiling the kettle and cooking the noodles before popping a container of noodles into Sam's hands. She kept her distance and took a seat on the chair in the corner of the room.

"It's okay, Alex. I don't bite, you know," Sam teased.

Alex blushed. "I know," she said before stuffing another plastic fork full of noodles in her mouth. "How is your leg?" She finally said.

"Tip-top Dr. Hunt. You did a mighty good job at removing that bullet, I'll tell you that. And, may I add, with no help from me at all. I'm impressed."

Alex smiled politely. "Have you managed to check the wound? I guess we'd have to clean it, no?"

"Already done. It looks as if I got lucky. It missed my femoral artery and the bone. The bullet would have fractured into pieces if it hit the bone or artery in which case I would have bled to death in minutes. Did you have to cut any muscle to get to the bullet?"

"Nope, it was tucked underneath. I couldn't get the pliers in so I pulled it out with my fingers. You passed out when I chucked the entire contents of that white bottle in the wound to stop the bleeding," pointing to the bottle with her fork.

"Well, whatever it was certainly did the trick. I managed to put weight on the leg already and got to the bathroom and back. You did an excellent job. I just have a tiny issue of concern, though."

Alex stopped eating and frowned. "What?"

Sam giggled. "Nothing too serious, you just shredded my jeans, so I have nothing to wear, that's all," casting his eyes to his torn denim pants lying on the chair behind her.

Her cheeks flooded a bright red as she realized what he was saying.

"You mean you're not wearing any pants under those covers?" Alex exclaimed in shock and horror.

"Starkers," Sam laughed sarcastically.

He loved teasing her and burst out laughing when she politely turned her back to him and covered her eyes.

"Relax, I still have my jocks on and there should be another pair in the trunk of the car. You do still have the car, don't you?"

Alex rolled her eyes and laughed. "Most of it. Speaking of, I narrowly escaped two Asians who tried to ram me off the road this morning, and *you* almost got killed last night. They're on the prowl for us. Whatever the reason, they won't stop until they find us. This village is too small for us to go unnoticed so I am of the opinion that we shouldn't attempt finding this man Yheng-Pho referred us to. We might not be so lucky a second time around. We should get out of here. I recall Yheng-Pho saying there was a pagoda in a town called Soc Trang. We should move our search there."

Sam pulled the map from his backpack next to him on the floor.

"You're right. It's not safe here. Soc Trang is south from here, about four hours by car. We should hang low here until nightfall and then make our way there. Did you hide the car?"

"I did. It's parked between the trees right outside our window. I shook them off my tail in the village, so we should be ok here for the next couple of hours. Get some rest."

CHAPTER TEN

Soc Trang, Southern Vietnam

It was close to 2 a.m. when they drove into Soc Trang. Sam slept most of the way while Alex kept her eyes peeled for anyone following them. They managed to flee undetected, shielded by the darkness of the night. The humidity dropped by several degrees making it also substantially cooler and more pleasant to travel in.

Unlike Tri Tong, this town was vastly smaller, covering only about forty-one miles versus the almost four hundred squared miles of the Tri Tong district. The streets were deathly quiet. There were no flashing neon lights and noisy clubs with half naked woman prancing around. The entire town seemed very much asleep. It shouldn't be too hard to find the pagoda, Alex thought. Most large cities have about five or six and they're easily visible from any vantage point.

Alex looked back at Sam as he lay on the backseat. He was still fast asleep. The painkillers the woman from the shop slipped into the brown paper bag knocked him out cold. For the most part, it should help his body heal; hopefully enough for him to walk. She was tired too. The events of the last forty-eight hours were wearing her down. She'd have to find a safe spot for them to pull over and gets some rest, but where? She zigzagged through the streets in search of a hotel, but everything was dark and closed. Scattered between the derelict buildings, several modern office and apartment blocks stuck out like sore thumbs. Being so near the South China Sea, it offered an excellent opportunity for trade and commerce companies to have their base.

Alex slammed on the brakes, nearly knocking over a stray dog. The streetlights weren't very bright, but she was certain she spotted a river up ahead. Upon closer inspection it was indeed; her tired eyes weren't deceiving her. She pulled over under the trees next to a ferry port. It was closed with nothing but an anchored ferryboat tied down to the small jetty. This would make an excellent place to park until morning.

Soft tapping against her car window woke them up the next morning. It was quite light already, and the hot sun broke through the partially shaded tree they had parked under. She rolled down her window to find a slightly bent over middle-aged Asian man ask if they needed the ferry.

"No-no, thanks," a half asleep Alex signaled with her hands to which the man signaled back for them to make way for the people behind them. Alex looked in her rear mirror spotting several commuters patiently sitting in a line behind them waiting for them to move onto the ferry.

"Oops, I'll move out the way...sorry!" Waving her hands apologetically in the air while starting the car and moving out of the line for the ferry.

"I thought that was room service," a sleepy Sam commented from the backseat.

"I'm afraid not. How's your leg?"

Sam sat up flexing his leg. "Remarkably fine, considering. I'll need to clean the wound and have a better look to be sure there's no infection but no complaints here. Where are you taking me for breakfast?"

"We need to find that temple and get cracking Sam. There's no time to waste. I need to know what precious Intel the scroll holds. We are no closer to finding the golden urn than what we were a month ago, and someone is prepared to kill us for it."

Her eye caught the orange fuel light on the dashboard.

"We need fuel. There's a gas station up ahead. We can ask for directions and grab something to go while we fill up."

Sam knew not to argue. She was right. They were in danger of something they had no part in.

"How did they know we had the scroll?" Sam asked still rubbing the sleep from his eyes.

"What do you mean?" A confused Alex replied.

"Well, think about it. How did these gangsters know we had something so valuable? The last place they chased after us was in Cambodia and I believe it was just a warning to get us to back off, but to follow us to Vietnam and then try to kill us? That is more than a mere warning. They knew we were onto something that would bring us all the way out here. No one knew we had a scroll that could be the hottest lead we've had all month."

"Except the patriarch, Roshi and..." she paused and caught Sam's eyes in the rearview mirror.

"Nah, there's no way Ollie would have said anything. Why would he take us all the way through a secret underground tunnel into a closed monastery, introduce us to the great senior patriarch and then have us followed? He could have simply asked the guru to show him the scroll again. He was certainly friendly enough with all those monks."

Alex tapped her fingers on the steering wheel. "I know. It doesn't make any sense. What we do know, however, is that he couldn't read it. So it's not entirely impossible to think that he needs us to decipher it, right? He could be using us, plain and simple as that."

The pair went quiet as they each digested the possibility of having been double-crossed by Ollie.

The gas station was thankfully already open when she pulled in next to a pump and started filling the car's empty tank. Several commuters whizzed by on their bikes. On the corner of the gas station, a young girl stood under an umbrella selling half-liter glass bottles of gasoline. Alex looked around. Nothing seemed out of the ordinary or suspicious, but Alex couldn't shake the feeling that they were being watched. Sam got out of the car and limped around to the trunk to retrieve the medical supplies.

"Be back before you know it," and disappeared into the men's room along the side of the building.

Alex flung her backpack over her shoulder and proceeded to the shop to settle the fuel bill. Another bell chimed as she stepped in through the door. The tiny shop was a flurry of chattering young adults collecting at the cold drinks and chocolate bars shelves. Alex grabbed some yogurt drinks and rolls, settled the bill and walked back to the car in time to see Sam shuffling from the bathroom.

"How's the wound?" Alex asked in passing.

"We're good to go. Let's find that temple."

The shop owner's directions took them through the village streets to the other side of the town. With the sun illuminating the outskirts of the village they spotted a solitary temple against the backdrop of the lush green hill and adjacent rice fields with ease.

Unlike the temple in Cambodia, this one, much to Sam's delight only had ten steps. Something he was secretly praying for in the bathroom while dressing his wound. It was much smaller in size and not remotely as attractive or impressive as the Oudong temple, which was built entirely from polished white marble. Instead, it had three tiers with multiple eaves and wholly constructed from ordinary bricks. The clay tile roof was a bright red that lit up like a candle when the sun shone through the overhangs. Each soffit adorned a brightly colored blue and red dragon draped along the edge of the roof making it impressive in its own right. Bright white pillars painted with turquoise and gold dragons, of which the tails twirled around the post, held up the first tier. At the foot of each post were several clay pots with the yellowest of yellow flowers growing from it. On either side of the staircases, which ran all around the squared building, more dragons guarded the steps, and more yellow flowerpots proudly invited visitors in. A much smaller Buddha statue made from white stone held several tiny babies and children in his arms. At its crossed legs were trays of incense and fresh flowers.

With not a single tourist in sight, the atmosphere was magical as they took in the full splendor of the majestic temple. Alex helped Sam up the steps through the double wooden doors that stood wide open. A young monk child, roughly around ten years old who had been tending to the shrine's flowers and candles in the center of the room, jumped up and rushed toward them. His friendly open face beamed with excitement as he greeted them in perfect English with tiny folded hands under his chin.

"Good morning Sir.,Madam. Can I give you each a candle?" Rushing back to the shrine to fetch it before they had a chance to answer him.

They didn't have the heart to disappoint the enthused child by declining the candles so, with a smile, accepted his gracious offering.

"Thank you, young man," Sam answered. "How old are you?"

The boy answered politely. "Nine, Sir, and you?"

Alex giggled, ready to dismiss him and get on with finding someone who could translate the scroll but Sam patiently answered, "Thirty-four and she's twenty-eight."

"That's old," the friendly boy replied innocently.

"You think so?" Sam continued happily.

"Yes, you are already limping."

Sam burst out laughing. "You're right. I should take better care of myself. What about her though? You think she's old?"

"Oh stop it," Alex cut in before the boy could answer and threw Sam a stern look. "You're only as old as you feel and I feel very young."

"You sound like my grandfather. He speaks like that too," the boy cheekily answered back which drove Sam to chuckles.

Alex was less amused. "And where is this wise grandfather of yours, young man? Is he around? We need his help."

The boy didn't hesitate. "Come, follow me. He's not very busy today. He is the wisest man you will ever meet. He will change your life forever," the boy said confidently.

They followed the energetic young boy outside and around the back of the temple. A narrow path between tall fruit trees and vegetable patches eventually brought them to a conservative looking wooden house next to a lily pad pond.

"Wait here," the boy instructed and disappeared into the house.

Several minutes later an elderly monk appeared. It was easy to see they were related. He had the same friendly open face as the boy, and though decades older, shared as much energy and enthusiasm for their surprise visitors.

Alex and Sam instantly bowed and greeted him to which he appreciatively responded. At his side, the young boy waited excitedly.

"Good morning, venerable Sir," Alex spoke. "I am Alex Hunt and this is Sam Quinn. We are British archaeologists and have acquired an ancient scroll, which we need to have translated. We were hopeful that you might be able to assist us, please?"

The boy's grandfather folded his hands behind his back and sized them up and down. What seemed like an hour of uncomfortable, silent surveillance, he finally spoke.

"Please come in," and turned back into the house.

The young boy's eyes lit up like fireworks and grabbed Sam's hand pulling him excitedly into his grandfather's house.

Inside, the home was cozy and very welcoming. Not at all what they had expected. Though small, it was open and flowed comfortably from one room to the next. They were quickly offered to take a seat on proper chairs, much to Sam's relief who desperately needed to rest his leg, and moments later the young boy placed a tray with fresh tea in front of them.

"Can you show me the scroll, please," the monk asked.

"Well, Sir, it's a photograph of the scroll. We weren't permitted to remove it from the monastery where it is at," Alex answered pulling the photos from the brown envelope in her backpack.

The monk nodded in acceptance and asked her to put it on the table. It wasn't considered appropriate for a monk to directly receive anything from a female.

He took several minutes to inspect the photographs, looking up at Alex and Sam multiple times in between as if to seek reassurance that they were trustworthy. His gentle voice instructed his grandson to do something who promptly jumped up and disappeared into the other room. Moments later the boy excitedly returned with an enormous parcel that made him look even smaller than his nine-year-old frame. It wasn't the first time Sam and Alex had seen a package like this one. They had seen it at the Oudong temple in Cambodia when they first arrived at the mountain shrine to inspect the crime scene. Alex felt her heart beating out of her chest. If this monk had the same sacred book with gold ink, then they were most definitely leaving there with something worthwhile. Could it be this boy's grandfather would be able to translate the scroll? She could hardly contain her excitement and squeezed her hands between her knees. Sam exchanged an equally excited look as they watched the monk untie the bound book and flip several banana leaf pages over before stopping somewhere in the middle of the book.

The boy hurriedly moved the tea tray to a nearby table and helped his grandfather place the open book in the center of the coffee table. Alex and Sam leaned over to take a closer look. The writing on the pages was identical to that of the scroll.

Alex gasped in excitement and knelt next to the table. "No way! This is it! It's identical," comparing the photo to the banana leaf page.

"I told you my grandfather was the wisest man on earth," the boy said proudly.

"Indeed you did, young man," Sam said patting the boy's shaven head. "Something tells me you are fast becoming as wise a man as your grandfather."

Undeterred by the bonding that was taking place next to her, Alex looked up at the monk.

"Sir, are you able to please tell us what the scroll says? We need to know what is written here. We would be most appreciative."

Something in the older monk's demeanor had changed. He was no longer suspicious of them. Instead, he grinned broadly and sat forward in his chair.

"But of course! If my great patriarch brother trusted you enough to show you the scroll, then I will do anything I can to help you."

A stunned Alex looked at him. "How did you know who showed it to us?"

"My dear British archaeologist, I wasn't born yesterday. There is only one brother in the entire world that holds this scroll. Many of the holy Buddha's teachings were written in the same language and shared across the world, but this scroll was written with one purpose."

Alex couldn't believe her ears. She knew this was to become the breakthrough in their hunt for the elusive golden urn. Alex could barely breathe as she sat waiting in anticipation for him to speak. Mesmerized by the events unfolding before her, she grabbed Sam's hand and squeezed it tight, catching the boy's attention.

"Are you married?" the boy asked.

Alex, whose gaze was fixed on the older man's lips embarrassingly snatched her hand back. She wasn't aware that she had been holding Sam's hand. "No," she blurted out. "We are very old friends."

The boy looked even more puzzled. "Friends don't hold hands," he said cheekily.

Sam looked at the boy and smiled mischievously.

"Perhaps you can advise me on how I would go about changing that?" Sam asked the boy as he flashed Alex a teasing smile.

Alex blushed bright red and sat back down in her chair. Ignoring Sam's feeble conversation with the boy, she shuffled uncomfortably.

"Ahem, sir please continue. What is written in the scroll?"

The monk smiled, his eyes sparkling like diamonds. "Yield to your heart, Miss. It will bring you great joy in life."

"I couldn't agree more," Sam chirped.

Alex jumped up, annoyed at the situation and walked around stopping behind her chair. "Really Sam?" she asked sarcastically. "We don't really have time for this, you know. Stop the silly games and let's get on with it please?"

The boy and his grandfather giggled, entirely amused by Alex scolding Sam.

"Okay okay, I'll back off, for now."

Sam threw his hands in the air, giving the boy a wink. "Sir," he continued with a straight face, "please do continue. This matter is of great importance to my friend here, and we could really do with your help to resolve the issue."

The monk looked up at Alex who by now was greatly frustrated.

"There were an elite few scribes in the world who were skilled to write like this. Royal elders passed down the honor, and scribes were hand selected by the ranking monk. The skill was strictly taught from scribe to scribe in closed teaching sessions. Most scrolls were used for reverent teachings, recording holy prayers and historical events, mostly on banana leaves. But this scroll is different. The leaves of the Buong tree preserved any writings longer than the banana leaves. It was reserved for communications only between the kings so this is a very important scroll. You can also see the symbol here," pointing to a small triangle in the top corner. "This was the unique signature of the Royal scribe."

Alex hastened around her chair and knelt next to the table to get a better look.

"What does it say?" she asked.

"It is a map."

Alex caught her breath in her throat. "A map! To where?"

"They were instructions to the Royal family on where to hide the sacred golden urn."

"You mean to say that the rumors are true? The urn that was stolen last month was in fact counterfeit?" Alex exclaimed and shot a surprised look at Sam who, by now, was also on the edge of his seat.

The monk nodded.

"But why? I don't understand, Sir. Why would they use a counterfeit Urn and hide the original one?"

"Simple, for the very reason it now got stolen," the elder answered. "To keep it safe and protected so it can be passed down through the Royal family."

"They know? The king knows this?" Alex said softly.

"But of course, my dear. He would not be a king worthy of his honor if he didn't guard this secret with his life. Unfortunately, when the Khmer Rouge infiltrated Cambodia, the second part of the scroll perished in a fire when they burned down the royal palace."

Sam, who had been quietly listening, cut in, "There was a second part of the scroll. Of course! It all makes sense now. That's why they hired us. With the second scroll destroyed the authentic urn will be lost forever unless we find it."

Alex leaned back in her chair to contemplate the urn's fate. She jumped up and started pacing the room.

"We need to find it, that's all. If we have the first scroll, we might be able to figure out the rest. Please, sir. What *exactly* does it say?"

The monk sat forward and picked up the photograph.

> Where the three kings sleep
> the guardian of the ancient world sits at their feet.
> Follow the teaching to where the sun's rays meet,
> Beware the serpent's tongue! It is a trap. Steer
>   clear
> and follow the map.
> The fire is your ally, it will light the way
> Keep to the center until you reach the clay

The monk placed the photograph back on the table and folded his hands in his lap.

Alex stopped pacing. "That's it? There's nothing else?" Alex asked to which the monk merely nodded and smiled.

Alex looked questioningly at Sam.

"Don't look at me for answers. It seems we have our work cut out for us," Sam said.

Alex started pacing the room again, chewing her thumbnail. "It could be anywhere. Where would we even start?"

The monk got up and walked over to her. "Be still and let your heart show you the way. Something tells me you will find what you seek when you stop thinking."

"Thank you, Sir," Alex replied. "We are most grateful. We will do our best to honor the king in our pursuit. Who knows? We might join you again soon for another cup of tea."

Sam got up and limped across the room to join them. The monk whispered something to the boy who left the room and promptly returned handing his grandfather an odd looking cane. The monk looked at Sam and handed him the walking stick.

"A wise man will always escape death, but a foolish man goes at it unprepared."

In that moment, Sam and Alex knew the man's wisdom far exceeded the obvious. Somehow he knew they were under threat and humbly accepted his gift.

Sam turned to the boy and placed his hands on his shoulder. "And you, young man, were entirely correct. Your grandfather is indeed the wisest man on earth. Make sure you follow his every word so you can inherit some of his wisdom, okay? Thank you for your help."

The boy beamed with pride and satisfaction.

"Yes, thank you indeed, little man, "Alex added.

CHAPTER ELEVEN

Phnom Penh, Cambodia

The trip back to their hotel in Phnom Penh was entirely dominated by discussions over the golden urn and the urgency around finding the bona fide one. Alex and Sam recited the scroll's riddle over and over in an attempt to decipher the clues. Excitement poured from every cell in Alex's body. Even while Sam nodded off from the painkillers, Alex continued to repeat the riddle out loud, but nothing sounded even vaguely familiar as to where they should start.

They arrived back at the hotel well into the evening and agreed to meet up for a late dinner to continue working on the clues. The hotel restaurant had already closed for the night, so they followed the main road along the river to a nearby local restaurant. Sam found his cane to be a welcome aid, inspecting it properly for the first time when they sat down at their table.

"I don't think I've ever seen anything quite like this," he commented. "It is most unusual, don't you think?"

Alex took the walking stick and inspected the odd-looking head of the dragon handle. It was entirely black apart from the gold dragon's tail that was coiled around the rod.

"Quite remarkable indeed. Now let's get back to business, shall we?" handing the cane back to Sam and flipping open her laptop. "Let's start at the beginning. The first line read '*Where the three kings sleep*'."

Her fingers frantically danced over the keyboard as she searched for possible locations.

"You will not believe how many kings there were. It could be any of them," she said annoyed.

"Where would they 'sleep'? In the Royal Palace perhaps?" Sam asked.

"Their bedrooms? But they're all dead," Alex replied.

"Their graves! Get it? They're asleep. In their graves," Sam yelled across the table. "Where were the kings buried when they died? Look for a Royal graveyard or something."

"Brilliant!" Alex hit the keys again before slumping disappointingly back in her chair. "None of them were buried. They didn't believe in burials. They were all cremated."

Sam pondered as he stuck a mouthful of noodles in his mouth. "Okay, so where were their ashes strewn?"

Alex turned to the search engine again. "All over the place, it seems. They were placed in stupas for the people to worship at."

"So in shrines, right?"

"Yup, shrines and there are many all over Cambodia."

"Okay, but Phnom Penh was the capital city, so it's fair to say it's somewhere here. How many stupas with king's ashes are around the city?"

"No way!" Alex shouted. "I don't believe it!"

"What? What is it?" Sam called watching as Alex's fingers moved faster over the keys. "WHAT? Speak up, woman."

"We were right there, Sam! It's the Oudong temple! It had three stupas, remember? Each stupa holds the ashes of a king. Look here," turning the laptop sideways so Sam could see more clearly.

"It says here, the first stupa is the North-Western one called Damrei Sam Poan and was built by king Chey Chetha II who ruled from1618 to 1626. He built it for the ashes of his predecessor, king Soriyopor, who was the founder of Oudong. The second stupa is Ang Doung. This was king Norodom's father. This stupa was built by him in 1891 and houses the ashes of king Ang Duong who ruled from 1845 to 1859. The South-Eastern of the three stupas is Mak Proum which is the funeral stupa of king Monivong who ruled from 1927 to 1941."

"That certainly fits the dates perfectly. You are brilliant Alex Hunt, you know that?" an impressed Sam called out. "Now we just have to figure out where the sun's rays meet."

"Sunrise or sunset and 'meet' with what?" Alex responded taking a bite of food for the first time that evening.

"Let's go there first thing tomorrow morning and have a look around. The next part of the clue is 'the guardian of the ancient world sits at their feet'. If we can figure out who the guardian of the ancient world is and at whose feet he is sitting, it might somehow bring us one step closer to finding the place where the sun's rays meet. I think this calls for a toast, don't you?" a cheery Sam announced as he called the waiter over.

Alex closed her laptop and finished her meal, unable to stop smiling or hide her excitement. The restaurant was completely empty and it was by now, close to midnight already.

"We should probably get back to the hotel and get some sleep. Tomorrow might be a busy day," Alex said. "Besides, I don't think it would be wise to drink while medicated. The mere thought of having to carry you is utterly daunting," she joked.

They were both in high spirits. It was the first taste of success since they had arrived in Cambodia. Alex shuffled excitedly on the chair.

"Do you realize how incredible it would be when we discover the original golden urn? Something no one even knew existed. We will go down in the history books, Sam!"

"I can see the headlines — Renowned archaeologists discover ancient lost golden urn!" Sam played along as they got to their car.

Moments later Alex's shrill screams echoed through the dark as two masked men picked her up and pulled her into a black van. Before Sam could stop them, he felt the painful blow to the back of his head seconds before everything went black.

When Sam came to it was pitch black. His eyes were open, yet he couldn't see a thing. When he tried lifting his hand to his face he couldn't and instantly realized his hands were bound above his head. Still disorientated he was aware that he was standing—just. Fighting the throbbing pain in the back of his head, he turned his head to find Alex.

"Alex," he called out but she didn't answer. Was it possible they hit her over the head too, and she was still unconscious? He focussed his eyes in a futile attempt to see better through the absolute darkness, but his eyes painted murky images of nothingness before him.

"Alex, can you hear me?" he tried again. "Are you here?" Still, there was no reply. All he heard was his voice bouncing hollow sounds off the walls. It confirmed what he already suspected, that he wasn't outside. It was hot and humid, and he became aware of the faint dripping of a tap somewhere in the background. Angst gripped at his throat as he tried to free his hands from the suspended rope above his head but it was too tight. Suddenly becoming aware he was shirtless, he then lifted his one knee to feel if he had his pants on. He did, but he wasn't wearing any shoes. Underneath his feet, the floor was wet and felt like concrete. He had no idea how long he had been hanging there or where Alex was. Deciding he'd have to rely on his other senses he closed his eyes and focussed his hearing on the surroundings, turning his head slowly from side to side. A dog was barking outside in the distance behind him. The dripping tap splashed onto the floor somewhere on his right. The tin roof made a rhythmic drumming sound. It was raining. He pondered whether the dripping tap wasn't perhaps a leak in the roof which would explain why the floor was wet. His mind trailed to his arms that had no feeling left in them. His medical background told him that he had to have been hanging for several hours for that to occur.

The darkness made him dizzy but he continued to look around for any objects that might give away his location. High above his head a small beam of moonlight was just visible in the roof making it obvious that it was nighttime. That meant that, if they had been captured just past midnight, it was entirely possible that it was around three or four a.m. The dog barked again. He turned his head toward the sound and was certain he heard footsteps coming from outside somewhere. He listened intently but couldn't be sure. His thigh hurt a lot since the painkillers had worn off and, desperate to know where Alex was, he called out to her again, but still, there was no reply. Fear flooded his mind. What if they killed her? He pushed the thought aside. It didn't make sense. If anything, they would kill him. She would be too valuable in helping them find whatever it was they were after. Deciding to cling to his theory, he wiggled his bound wrists in an attempt to pull his fists through the loops of the rope. The scruffy rope chafed at his sweaty skin leaving an intense burning behind, but he pushed on and kept at it for several more minutes. He had to keep trying if he were to get out of there. For all he knew they intended on leaving him there to rot to death.

A couple of hours later, the moonlight through the roof made way for a faint beam of sunlight and the hard rain from earlier had stopped. His wrists were raw, but he had wriggled enough that the cord was not as tight as before. He no longer registered the immense pain coming from his flesh or aching armpits.

The complete darkness around him had somewhat dissipated into a dark grey shade that allowed him to see faint images of something resembling a chair several feet in front of him. From what he could tell he appeared to be in some sort of warehouse. He looked up at his hands. Streams of blood from his raw wrists had trickled down his arms to where it now rested on his shoulders. He was exhausted. Though there was a slight improvement in visibility, he still couldn't see or hear Alex anywhere around him. The dog wasn't barking either. Fatigue overcame him, and he stopped wriggling, just for a moment. He wiped the sweat from his brow with his shoulder and relaxed his chin on his chest. He would give his hands a break and then try again, even if the rope ripped away any remaining flesh from his bones.

His moment of rest was short lived when the clanging sound of a padlock being unlocked was echoed through the emptiness around him. Someone was there. Could it be Alex coming for him? He squinted his eyes toward the noise in an attempt to see but it was still too dark. The door screeched open and allowed the bright daylight to light up the narrow doorway at the far end of the warehouse. He narrowed his eyes in response to shield the bright light from his eyes all the while refusing to look away. The shadowy silhouettes of what looked like three men moved through the opening toward him. His heart rate quickened as realization struck that they were the kidnappers. Within seconds a piercing light from a spotlight hit him full in his face. He jerked his head away on impulse and tightly shut his eyes. It was done with intent, blinding him from their identity. The metal feet of a chair being put down sounded on the concrete floor and Sam fought hard to take control of his raging emotions.

"Good morning, Dr. Quinn," an authoritative male voice resounded.

Sam had no intentions of being polite by reciprocating the greeting from a man who spoke perfect English with only the slightest Asian accent.

"Where's Alex?" Sam responded, surprised at how weak his voice sounded in comparison.

"She's safe," the man answered, "for now."

Sam went weak. "I want to see her."

"I'm afraid that is entirely dependent on you, Dr. Quinn."

Unsure of what he meant, Sam kept quiet and instinctively tugged at the rope around his hands.

"Oh save your energy, Dr. Quinn. You are going to need it. Unless of course you decide to cooperate with us."

Sam's heart skipped several beats as he contemplated the significance of keeping the scroll's content secret versus saving Alex's life. Knowing her, she would rather die a thousand deaths than allow a relic to fall into the hands of evildoers. Could he, on the other hand, permit himself to have her killed by refusing to cooperate?

"What do you want?" Sam said softly.

"It's really very simple, Dr. Quinn."

Sam cringed at this man's politeness.

"We need the content of the scroll," the man continued. "Tell us what it says, and we will let you both go."

Judging from the conditions surrounding his capture Sam instinctively knew they'd never let them go after they got their own way. Even without their identities known, they would undoubtedly kill them both.

"I need to see Alex first, see if she's okay," Sam gambled.

The man laughed sarcastically, "Dr. Quinn. I am not in the business of idle threats. This here is not a negotiation. You either comply or you don't and bear the consequences. Your decision."

Sam heard the chair scraping ever so slightly on the floor followed by footsteps moving away from him. Deciding to play his bluff, Sam remained silent. They would be back to try again, he thought. He guessed they would work the same maneuver with Alex, but knowing how protective over relics she can be, they stood little to no chance of succeeding. He knew her well enough to be convinced of that. As long as they didn't hurt her, he would wager that the man would not succeed.

The spotlight still blinded him, so he kept his eyes closed. Seconds later he felt a hard punch to his stomach leaving him gasping for air. A second and third punch followed in quick succession. He hung from the rafters unable to breathe; like a human piñata about to explode all over the floor. He heard footsteps moving in behind him before he felt another blow against his kidneys. The dull thrust filled his mouth with blood. His feet were too numb to help him regain his balance, and he swung forward and spun around. With the spotlight behind him, he caught a glimpse of his attacker for the first time. There was just one. The other one might have left with the man in charge. Could he somehow muster the strength to use his suspended fists as support and kick his attacker in the hope of knocking him out? Then what? He'd still be hanging unable to free himself. If he failed at knocking him out, it might just anger him. Sam decided to tough it out. He pulled his stomach muscles tight as he prepared for another punch, but instead heard the man walking away. Shortly after, he heard the door open before the spotlight switched off and the padlock clicked back in place.

The warehouse was dark again, and he blinked several times to help his eyes become accustomed to the darkness. When his eyesight adjusted, he squinted at the crevice in the roof again. The sun's rays shone slightly brighter now bringing into focus the expanse of the structure. The warehouse was entirely empty with nothing but the single chair in front of him. Still struggling to catch his breath and recover from his beating, he turned around slowly. There was a tiny window in the roof above the rafters that allowed more light in. It was already sweltering and humid during the night, so without any ventilation, it would soon become a sauna that would drain him of any water he might still have left in his exhausted body. Logic told him that they wouldn't return until nightfall to continue preventing their identity from being known.

He spat a ball of bloody saliva onto the floor and wiped the corner of his mouth against his shoulder. His breathing had returned to normal, but the dull aching on his kidneys remained and he no longer had any feeling in his arms. He looked up at his bound hands to assess the lacerations on his wrists. The rope had been twisted around his hands several times finished off by a double knot. The more he pulled down at it, the tighter the knots became. Clever, he thought. He tried not to hang on the rope, robbing him of an immense amount of willpower and strength. He stood upright and tried to stand on his toes, but his legs were just as weak. Still trying to recover from the bullet wound, it throbbed under the strain of having been vertical for so long.

He tried once more and wriggled his hands as his fingers worked the knots. It loosened, somewhat, but not enough to come undone. Fighting with all his strength, his toes eventually gave way, and the rope pulled tight again. If ever there were a time he could cry, it would have been then. He had only ever cried once in his entire life, and that was when his little sister exhaled her last breath. She was twelve at the time. He was fifteen. The doctors had done everything they could, or so they said. They stopped fighting for her. She couldn't fight anymore either. Leukemia had drained her of any existence of life. Life. It was never the same after she died. Dad threw himself into his veterinary practice, and four-legged patients as a way of coping with her death and Mom entered just about every baking competition and homemaker's fair in the district. They all aimed at staying as busy as possible to avoid being in their much too silent house for any extended periods of time.

Sam felt a tear gently roll down his cheek. Perhaps that was why his parents pushed him toward becoming an oncology doctor. Why they were so adamant, he followed in the family tradition of medicine even though it was too late. What good would that have done? Their daughter and his only sibling were gone forever. He tried. God knows he tried. In spite of the fact that he had finished top of his class and achieved the highest recognition, his heart had lost a piece that could never be mended.

The sharp squeak of a rat scuffling from underneath an old crumpled newspaper that lay in the middle of the floor toward the door jerked him back to the present. Alex was out there somewhere being tortured by these scumbags. For all he knew she was beyond her point of tolerance and depending on him to save her. Hell will freeze over before he let her down and lost her too. He will fight with whatever was left in him. He had to keep trying with the knots, even if it killed him.

CHAPTER TWELVE

H er head was pounding, and the room spun like a merry-go-round as Alex sat up in a completely unfamiliar bed. The bitter taste on her tongue and her dry mouth revealed that she had been drugged. She recalled being grabbed outside the restaurant and feeling the sharp pain of a needle in her neck, but nothing else. Gathering her orientation, she looked around the small room. She didn't see Sam anywhere. Did they only take her, she suddenly doubted.

The room resembled that of a dreary basement. There was a steel spiral staircase in the middle of the room and several boxes and old pieces of furniture stacked in the corner under the stairs. It was dark and smelled of dirty laundry, yet there was no washing in sight. Careful not to lose her balance Alex slowly got up to walk to the stairs but was instantly yanked back onto the bed. She looked down at her arm to see a rusty metal cuff around her wrist. A chain was attached to the cuff and ran along the floor underneath her bed. She bent down to follow the chain where it stopped at the foot of her bed against the wall. Attached to this end of the chain was another cuff fastened around a steel pipe that had been bolted into the brick wall. She pulled her arm in a wishful attempt to break free delivering no surprise that nothing happened. She was chained down like a caged circus animal.

Fear gripped her insides as she surveyed the room for any signs of Sam. Apart from her bed, there was nothing else in the space that indicated he was or had ever been there. She searched for a window, but this too delivered no results. Her watch showed it was about four hours after she was kidnapped, so she had been knocked out for most of the night. She spotted a small server with a glass of water on the floor next to her feet. The tray was red with several small images of white and gold flowers printed all over it. It was typical of the cheap kitchen paraphernalia sold at almost every corner market. At least it proved she might still be in Cambodia and hadn't been flown off to a country in the middle of nowhere. She licked her dry lips. Drinking from the glass of water was very tempting, but she couldn't help wonder if the drink might be spiked. She picked it up and held it up against the light of the small bedside lamp that was on a crate next to the bed. There was no visible evidence of any particles or discoloration; at least not to her naked eye. It also didn't have any odor. If they wanted her dead they could have killed her already, so worst case scenario, it would knock her out for another couple of hours. She took a small sip and swirled it in her mouth. It was tasteless, so she gulped down the glass, sat back and waited to see if it had any effect. Several minutes went by, and nothing happened. Satisfied she would survive it she started fiddling with the cuff and chain again. The chain was no more than ten feet in length, at best, which offered no opportunity for her to reach the bottom of the staircase and even if she could, then what? She was a sitting duck waiting for whatever they were planning. Her mind trailed to Sam, hoping he would be okay wherever he was. If her kidnappers only took her, he would have sought help from the Commissioner-General by now, and they'd be out looking for her. On the other hand, if they captured him too, he'd be somewhere locked up in a room also. She knocked on the wall behind her bed.

"Sam! Are you there?"

She listened, knocked and called several more times, but the bare brick wall stared back at her in silence. Her mind pushed away from the nagging thought of Sam lying dead next to the car on the restaurant's curb. He was tall and athletic and even with his injured leg he would have fought them off for sure. Sam had become so much more than just a colleague. They were friends who depended on each other, and right now she depended on him to save her. The sudden realization that perhaps he could be worse off than her and depending on her to rescue him instead paused her trailing thoughts. She knelt down on the floor next to the bed and followed the chain to where it was fastened to the other steel cuff around the gutter pipe. The bed wasn't fixed to the floor, so she pulled the shackle across the concrete and slipped it out from under the two legs of the bed allowing the chain to move freely up the pipe above her bed. It stopped at a join about halfway between the floor and the low ceiling. The join was fastened to the brick wall and covered by a metal clasp that was bolted in by two rusted screws. She yanked the chain back in an attempt to loosen the pipe from the wall. Fine cement dust escaped from the screws in the wall. It could work if she kept at it, she thought, so she yanked harder. The cuff clanged against the steel pipe and set off quite a racket. A cloud of dust puffed into the air. Her pulse raced uncontrollably, exhilarated at the prospect of breaking the conduit and having an opportunity to escape.

A sharp burning sensation radiated from under the rusty cuff around her wrist. Her skin was red and inflamed from the friction, but she couldn't stop now. She had a chance, and she would have to take it. Another hard tug on the pipe and one screw popped halfway out of its socket. She gasped in excitement over her success that encouraged her to wrap her hands directly around the steel tube to pull it from the wall. Hearing a noise coming from the top of the staircase she froze. Someone was unlocking the door. She hurriedly pulled the chain back down to the floor and underneath the feet of the bed, pushed the screw back into the wall and sat down on her bed just in time to see a pair of black combat boots come down the spiraled steps. Her heartbeat echoed in her ears as she struggled to regain her composure. Moments later a man dressed from head to toe in black appeared at the end of the stairs. His face was covered with a black mask, and he didn't utter a single word. In his hand, he carried another small tray with a bowl of noodles and a glass of water and swapped it with the other one on the floor. Alex caught her breath as she spotted the black tattoo on the back of his neck. It was a scorpion similar to the one Sam said he had noticed on the biker's neck. Could it be the same man? Alex tensed up and leaned away from him toward the end of the bed. If this were the same man, he would have a score to settle with her for throwing him off the motorbike and almost killing him.

"Where am I?" She braved.

The man didn't answer or even look at her. Alex could hardly breathe, but she held firm even though her body was trembling with fear. She clenched her fists together to hide her shaking hands.

"Hey I'm speaking to you! Where am I and where is Sam? I demand that you tell me."

The man who had already walked toward the staircase stopped and turned to face her. His black eyes stared at her intently without answering before ascending the stairs, sending a shiver down her spine. The door locked behind him and she was left alone again.

She stared down at the bowl of noodles and then glanced at her watch. It was five thirty a.m. They were keeping her alive and making sure she was nourished. Why? What did they want from her? She wasn't hungry, but she didn't know what lay ahead. The thought that the food might be poisoned or drugged crossed her mind again. Nothing had happened after the water she drank earlier. The food should be adequate too, so she decided to eat, all the while looking back at the loose screw in the wall. She needed to be smart about this. Should she manage to successfully free herself from the pipe, she'd still have the chain cuffed to her hand and the door at the top of the stairs to unlock. Any kidnapper with half a brain cell would have at least one man guarding the exit. She scoured the room for some sort of weapon that could work. There was nothing she could see. It was hardly surprising they would leave anything that might pose as a weapon.

She slumped back onto the bed and decided she'd wait. Sooner or later they would be back to make their demands known.

Her thoughts were barely a memory when she heard the key in the lock at the top of the stairs. Her eyes remained fixed on the steps which this time, presented two pairs of legs descending. They were both dressed identically; black pants, shirts, and masks. Alex felt her body tense up as the two men approached her and proceeded to unlock the cuff around her wrist. The one with the black eyes paused and stared at her red chafed skin before looking directly at her. She bit the inside of her bottom lip, careful not to show any fear. The men flanked her on both sides and grabbed her by her arms before shoving her toward the stairs. Neither spoke. Eager to get out of the room she didn't resist and climbed the metal steps to where she opened the door at the top of the stairs. A third masked man stopped her dead in her tracks. The door had opened up to a corridor. To her right was a kitchen and at the end of the passage to her left, several more doors; possibly bedrooms. She paused to silently question if Sam was likely to be in any of those rooms but found herself being pushed toward the kitchen that was small and poorly decorated with the most ghastly bright green walls. Days worth of dirty dishes lay in the sink, and the four-seated round dining table in the center of the room displayed ivory colored domino-like game pieces of a traditional Asian pastime. Evidence that the three men were living upstairs confirmed that there would have been no way on earth she would have been able to escape. She was more likely to have been killed trying.

They pushed her past the table and out the other end of the kitchen into an equally dated lounge. The television in the corner was tuned to a program showing two bloody men fighting in a ring circled by several spectators cheering them on. The commentary was in Mandarin. Alex relaxed slightly knowing now that she was still in Cambodia. The man with the black eyes pointed to one of the kitchen chairs he had placed in the middle of the lounge for her to sit. The second one tied both her hands behind her back while the third guard covered her eyes with a blindfold.

She didn't fight them off even though every fiber of her terrified body wanted to. Instinctively she knew this was in preparation for a meeting with the man in charge. She needed to know what they did with Sam and what they demanded of her.

With her eyes blinded she listened intently and heard the creaking of a door to her right followed by several footsteps shuffling on the wooden floor around her. She had been aware of the three guards so knew, at the very least, they were in the room, however, she had no idea how many other people had joined them. Several moments later, a voice cut through the silence.

"Well, well, well. Miss Hunt. The famous Alexandra Hunt."

Alex tensed at the calm male voice that spoke with a mocking tone across from her.

"What do you want?" she said with a voice that sounded grittier than usual trying her level best to hide her fear.

"Tst Tst Tst, that's hardly a polite way to welcome your business partner," the stranger continued.

"You're sorely mistaken, mister. I don't do business with people I don't trust or know," Alex bit back. There was something about this man's voice that was very recognizable. She just couldn't quite place the similarity.

"Well, my dear. I don't think you will have many choices in the matter. You see. I have something you want, and you have something I want."

The man kept quiet. Alex could only think of Sam. Her parents in all likelihood would be safely back home. Choosing not to take his bait she suppressed the instinct to answer. In some way she was grateful he could not see her eyes behind the blindfold. Equally, she wished she could see his so she could read his next move. Her stomach turned with fear that this man and his thugs might have hurt Sam, but she dared not show it.

"Oh come on Miss Hunt. Your silence is hardly going to sway me from getting what I want. Trust me. This is one bluff you don't want to call."

Alex felt her throat tighten. She knew she didn't have it in her to gamble with Sam's life or wellbeing.

"What do you want?" She answered with the slightest quiver in her voice.

"The location of the urn of course. Tell me where to find it, and I'll let you go."

"Where's Sam?"

"Dr. Quinn is...well, let's just say he's hanging on for you to give me what I want."

Alex couldn't move or speak. Her heart pounded in her chest. Stiffened with the knowledge that the kidnapper was indeed holding Sam captive, she contemplated her next move. Finding the golden urn, which they now knew was the authentic relic, was crucial. Its rightful place was back in the Royal family. Having it end up in the hands of criminals only meant trouble. She was torn between the fate of returning a two thousand five hundred year old lost relic and saving the life of her dearest friend and colleague.

Her mind was racing with scenarios. Perhaps they wouldn't kill Sam, after all, he was leverage. But every instinct of hers knew not to trust this man. He could be calling her bluff. It wasn't impossible to believe that Sam could have easily escaped or— she paused her thoughts for a brief moment—he could already be dead.

She took a deep breath and concluded that she would stand her ground and play it out as confidently as she possibly could.

"The urn is a sacred relic that belongs to the Royal family of Cambodia. You have no right to claim and abuse it to serve your malicious, selfish intentions. Besides, I don't have it."

She decided to hold back her plea for Sam's life to circumvent showing any vulnerability or weakness that could be exploited for his gain.

The man let out an arrogant laugh. "I am no man, ahem, or woman's fool, Miss Hunt. You have been given an ancient scroll which was reserved for secret communications between kings only. You cracked its code and now you know where to find the original golden urn."

Alex caught her breath in her throat. He knew! This man knew about the scroll and that she and Sam managed to translate its contents. How was that possible? As if a cloud lifted from her blinded eyes, in that instant, she knew. These guys were unmistakably the same people who had been following them around Cambodia and all the way to Vietnam. She frantically searched her memory for a clue as to whom this man might be. His voice was definitely familiar, but his accent wasn't. He wasn't Asian or British, yet he spoke fluent and perfect English. He was calm and over-confident. The faint smell of a cigar hung in the air. It was likely his. She detected the slightest whiff of cologne, but that could have been any of the guard's scents.

"I honestly don't feel it necessary to subject you to torture, Miss Hunt. Your colleague, on the other hand, I have no use for. So the choice is really yours. One way or another, my methods WILL get you to co-operate. I am a businessman, Miss Hunt, and I usually get my way. Prolonging it will just lead to innocent people getting hurt. It can all be prevented. Save your dearest Sam and us a lot of unnecessary time wasting and blood spill and give me the scroll."

Her bluff failed hopelessly, they had Sam, and if she didn't comply with his demands, he would be tortured and killed. Saving the precious gold relic wasn't anywhere as important as preserving Sam's life. She could live without the urn's discovery, but she couldn't live without Sam. She knew this now and impulsively wriggled her wrists in a futile attempt to loosen the tightly bound ropes.

As if to ensure she exerted sufficient authority to withstand this man's emotional blackmail, she straightened in the chair and replied,

"I don't have the scroll. We weren't allowed to take it."

She heard a shuffling from the couch opposite her where she guessed the kidnapper sat. Her answer apparently caught him by surprise. He was under the impression that she had the actual scroll. She should seize this opportunity and prey on his vulnerability, so she added.

"In fact, there are two scrolls. The second one burned in the fire when the Khmer Rouge attacked the Royal Temple. So you see,

Mr. whoever you are, there is no possible way the urn can be found. It is lost forever."

The room fell eerily silent. To the point where Alex wasn't even sure if there was anyone left in the lounge with her. Perhaps the shuffling wasn't his discomfort with her revelation but him leaving the room. She sat silently waiting it out. The knowledge that there was a second scroll needed to find the urn might have derailed the kidnapper's plans entirely. It could be her and Sam's saving grace. A flicker of enthusiasm bubbled within and gently pushed her fears aside. Could it be that his plan had backfired and he was now forced to let them go? He would have no further use for them. Likewise, he could just as quickly kill them both.

She was aware of someone breathing behind her. The cigar smell still hung in the air, thicker than before. She knew her kidnapper must still be there. She had a distinct feeling that he was watching her every move. Like a poker player surveying his opponent or a lion ready to charge. Either way, it was his move now.

The idea of being eyeballed by a criminal made her very uncomfortable, primarily because she couldn't see him from underneath the blindfold. She dared not show her fear now. If she could maintain her confidence, he would know she was telling the truth and that could mean the difference between life and death.

CHAPTER THIRTEEN

As if the kidnapper had read her mind, Alex heard the door he had entered the room with squeak open. Was he leaving? She listened but didn't detect it being shut behind him. She turned her head sideways to push her ear closer toward the entrance but got caught by surprise when one of the guards who had been behind her untied her hands. She was lifted to her feet, and the thought of escaping briefly crossed her mind. With her hands freed, she could elbow him off and make a run for the door. Her great escape was nothing more than a pipe dream when the guard pulled both her hands in front of her and tied them together. She swore under her breath for not grabbing the opportunity. Seconds later the blindfold was ripped off her face. Bright sunlight beamed through the open door forcing her to briefly shut and shield her eyes with her bound fists. There were two guards in front of her at the door and two behind her. Her stomach turned upside down. She would have stood no chance fighting off four armed guards in ninja suits.

Pushed from behind the thugs ushered her toward the open door.

"Where are you taking me?" She panicked.

They didn't answer. Instead, the men pushed her down the narrow garden path to the black minibus that stood parked on the curb in front of the house. Once inside and with the doors closed, she noticed that all the windows had been painted with a thin layer of black paint. Though the van wasn't completely dark inside, she couldn't see out at all. She had hoped she'd be able to detect her location. She turned toward the front window of the vehicle, but a black screen had also blocked this off. Disheartened she stayed seated on the floor facing the black screen. Two of the guards sat on either side of her, one of them holding the rope her hands were tied to. It was entirely possible that they were going to let her go and drop her off somewhere in a ditch by the river. *But what if they had no intentions on it at all?*

She closed her eyes and counted the seconds the van faced forward and how many times it changed gears. She listened for street and background noises, how often the vehicle turned left and how long before it turned right. In a desperate attempt, she memorized every move to the best of her ability. It was roughly ten minutes and several turns later when she heard more commuters and traffic than before followed by the disorderly shouting of a group of merchants. A strong fishy smell filled her nostrils. It rang familiar to her, very familiar in fact. It was the fish market in the center of the town. Excitement bubbled up from within. Her pulse quickened as she realized exactly where she was. Her senses were on high alert. She might not have been able to make use of her sight from inside this bus but she most certainly could use her other faculties to track her location.

❋

Her wristwatch indicated fifteen minutes of driving through the town and Alex had followed the route intently to where the vehicle eventually came to a halt. When they let her out she took it all in. They had parked in the middle of a deserted warehouse facility that appeared to be part of an abandoned factory plant of some sort. The area was deathly quiet apart from a fierce barking dog that was chained to the security fence. Just outside the enclosed space, a faded sign read Khyadamri Inc. in big black letters. The name didn't ring a bell with Alex at all, so she drew her attention toward the luxury black sedan that was stationed next to a warehouse behind them. The car didn't have any number plates or markings of any kind.

The hard tug of the rope around her wrists propelled her toward the storage facility behind the sedan. Her eyes concentrated hard on the tinted windows of the sedan in the hope of seeing who was inside, but apart from another ninja costumed driver, she saw no one else. Alex stumbled into a walk as the kidnappers dragged her past the parked car and through the warehouse door. Nothing she had ever experienced prepared her for what she caught sight of next. In the center of the dark warehouse, a bright spotlight illuminated the body of a man hanging from a suspended rope. His hands were tied to the cord above his head, and his limp body had been stripped of his shirt and shoes. The man wasn't moving. Alex couldn't quite see his face with his head bent down, but a horrid feeling gripped at the pit of her stomach. Her legs stopped moving as she stood staring across the dark storeroom. *NO! It couldn't be.*

The guards pushed her toward the dangling body and shoved her down on a chair directly in front of the man. Positioned lower, she could clearly see his face. The stabbing pain in her heart as she realized it was Sam knocked her breath away.

"Sam," she let out the faintest of cries.

Sam didn't move. Deep emotions of fear ripped through her quivering body.

"SAM!" she shouted loudly. "It's me, Alex!"

Sam lifted his head ever so slightly. Alex stared at his face. It was so badly beaten his eyes were practically swollen shut. Blood covered his mouth and had trickled down his neck onto his chest. Across his abdomen and ribs lay deep purple bruises. It was a ghastly sight Alex knew she would never forget.

"Sam, can you hear me?" She spoke gently, but before he could answer, she swung around to the guards who still stood firmly behind her.

"Let him down you bastards! Let him down!"

She banged her bound fists against the masked ninja's chest and kicked him in his shin. Within seconds the other guard's strong arms picked her up and shoved her back into the chair and tied her down.

"You won't get away with it you beasts! Let us go!" she screamed.

Sam let out a faint groan, "Alex."

Hearing Sam's voice instantly stopped her from fighting.

"Sam? Are you ok?" She asked.

He was barely alive. Sam groaned softly again in an attempt to speak.

"Don't worry Sam. I'm going to get us out of here. Hang tight," cringing as she realized the inappropriate double intent of her words. "Sorry! You know what I mean," she stumbled through her apology as she frantically looked from side to side for a way out. The spotlight behind her blinded her from seeing anything other than Sam's tortured body in front of her.

"Come out, you coward!" She shouted toward the door. "I know you're in here."

She tried shuffling the chair around, but it was too heavy for her to lift without the use of her hands. She shouted again.

"Hey! I know you're in here. Your fancy car is parked outside. I demand you let Sam go!"

Loud contemptuous applause pierced through the darkness behind her.

"This is quite the performance, Miss Hunt," the kidnapper said. "In fact, I could watch you squirm all day."

Alex turned her head toward him.

"Yeah well, I'd think twice about that if I were you. Show your face, you coward," she dared while trying to not let her shaking knees give away the terror that tortured her body inside.

The kidnapper laughed out loud. "You are hilarious, Miss Hunt, acting all tough with me. I don't think you quite understand the situation before you. Look at him. How long do you think your boyfriend will last, huh?"

Alex looked back at Sam who was barely conscious. His arms were pale as all the blood from his veins had been drained. His wrists exposed lines of raw flesh beneath the ropes in an obvious effort to fight his way out of the tightly bound ropes. He most certainly was too weak to fight anyone off, much less escape, but if there were one thing Alex knew, it was that Sam Quinn was far more resilient than his put together happy-go-lucky demeanor displayed. As if Sam read her thoughts, he pinned his swollen eyes directly to hers and gave her a faint smile. He still had fight left in him, and he knew Alex would fight to protect the relic until the very end.

Welcoming his silent encouragement, she proceeded with new vigor.

"He's not my boyfriend. Give it up. The golden urn will never be yours."

How long she could push her boundaries, she didn't know, but she would push however much the situation allowed. As long as Sam was still alive and able to fight, she couldn't back down.

The kidnapper snapped his fingers. From the corner of her eye, she spotted movement in the dark. Moments later, two more ninjas approached pulling a squeaky-wheeled trolley behind them. Once they stood in the light behind Sam, Alex noticed the car battery and bucket on top of the cart. At first, she didn't quite put the pieces together. Gold and blue sparks scattered through the murky shadows behind Sam. Horror paralyzed her body. Sam looked at her briefly before shutting his eyes and lowering his head to his chest. Tears flooded Alex's tormented eyes. Shocking prisoners into submission had been a torture method used for thousands of years. In his current condition, Sam would never survive it. It could kill him, and no matter how much she wanted to protect the sacred lost relic, she would never be able to live with herself if they killed him.

Alex drew back several sharp breaths in an attempt to suppress her sobs that threatened to overwhelm her entire body as the masked men threw a bucket of water over Sam's battered body and tortured him in front of her. She vomited across the floor between her feet and shut her eyes tight. Sam's agonizing screams bellowed through the empty warehouse before she could no longer stomach it.

"STOP! STOP!" she screamed.

They did, and she heard Sam breathe a massive sigh of relief in response. She cried uncontrollably as she watched his near life-less body dangle from the rafters.

"You can end all of this, Miss Hunt. Tell us where the urn is," the man's voice echoed from the back of the storeroom.

"Sam," she whispered through her sobs, ignoring the kidnapper's threats.

"Let him down," she cried which yielded no reaction whatsoever from the man at the back or his posse.

"I said, LET HIM DOWN!" spelling it out with emphasis.

The man snapped his fingers again to which his group of puppets promptly responded. She watched as they cut Sam's rope above his head and left him to slump down onto the wet concrete floor like a puppet without a string. A second later they cut the cord from her own hands. Freed from the chair Alex leaped forward and lifted Sam's head onto her lap. He still didn't move. She wedged her body in behind his torso to aid the blood flow into his arms and rubbed each arm vigorously. Yet he didn't wake up. If they murdered Sam, she would hunt them down until the end of the earth.

"You killed him, you evil bastard!" she screamed. "You killed him!"

Her voice broke off as the tears poured down her cheeks onto Sam's lifeless face. She didn't care now anymore. They could kill her too.

"I will NEVER give you what you want! Do you hear me? NEVER! You killed him, and I will die before I ever let your grubby, greedy paws near that urn!"

The man's fingers snapped again, and one of his ninjas walked up and launched a bucket of water at Sam's face, drenching Alex in the process. Sam jerked his head back and drew in a sharp breath.

"Sam! It's me, Alex. Can you hear me?"

Barely audible he whimpered in response.

"Sam! You're alive!" drying his face with the bottom of her T-shirt.

"He needs a doctor. You need to get him to the hospital," Alex demanded.

"Miss Hunt. I told you before. You are in no position to give me any demands. I want the urn, and you're going to help me get it. Your boyfriend is alive, for now, but only for as long as you co-operate. So, do we have an understanding or not?"

This time, Alex knew she couldn't call his bluff. This man, whoever he was meant business and he would stop at nothing to get what he wanted, even if it meant killing Sam.

"If you don't get a bed and food in here, I won't help you. I need to see that Sam is taken care of first. Then I'll help you."

"That settles it then," the man said snapping his fingers once more after which two of his men picked Sam up and another threw Alex over his shoulders.

"Put me down you imbecile!" Her fists hammered against the thug's back. "Where are you taking Sam? PUT ME DOWN!"

The men carried both her and Sam up a set of stairs to a small room in the ceiling of the warehouse. Alex watched as they placed Sam on a mattress on the floor and moments later a young timid looking female joined them and knelt next to Sam on the floor. With wide eyes, Alex stared at the young girl who couldn't have been older than fifteen. She looked fearfully at the guards, and Alex noticed several cut marks and old bruises on her arms and face. She had read of the child trafficking rings operating in the East, and it was nauseatingly evident this teenager was there under duress. Alex couldn't speak as the reality of her kidnapper's violent and criminal acts hit her. The youth gently started cleaning Sam's face and torso with soapy water and a clean towel. Sam let out soft groans as she sponged off his bruised and battered body.

"Sam, it will be okay. You're going to be okay," Alex managed to whisper.

Just then another young girl came into the room with a tray of noodle soup and water and proceeded to feed Sam.

Alex wasn't sure if she should be happy that Sam was being seen to or sad that these poor young girls were subjected to a despicable act of slavery.

Perhaps the ninja with the black eyes couldn't stomach it either because moments later he pulled Alex by her arm and shoved her toward the steps back down to the main level. They walked past the spot where Sam's body had been tortured, and Alex glanced at the bloodstained puddle in the middle of the floor.

"Now, Miss Hunt," the voice came again from the back. "I have kept my side of the bargain now it's your turn. Where is the golden urn?"

Annoyingly the man was right. He did keep his promise in taking care of Sam. There was no escaping this. She would have to comply if they were to ever leave there alive.

"How do I know you won't kill us after I tell you?" She challenged.

"You don't. I guess you have no choice but to trust me."

Alex didn't answer. In her head, her mind was working overtime to find a way out of this awful ordeal. The truth was that she didn't know where the urn was either. All she knew was the cipher from the ancient scroll, which would take them somewhere, but not to the final location of the urn. Without the second scroll, it might be entirely hopeless.

"I can see you're not easily convinced, Miss Hunt. So, I'll make you a deal. You can lead my men, and once you find my relic, I will give you the address to this location, and you can come back for Dr. Quinn."

The man's voice sounded arrogant and filled with deceit, but she was backed into a corner. If she went with him, and somehow managed to escape, she knew she'd be able to find this warehouse on her own to save Sam.

"Fine, but I can't guarantee anything. Like I said before. There was a second scroll which burned..."

"Yes, yes, Miss Hunt, so you keep saying. I do happen to also know that you possess somewhat of a reputation for finding lost relics without any maps, so I'll take my chances. Besides, I think I have made it abundantly clear that Sam will die if you don't help me find that urn."

Alex looked up at the little room where the young girls were attending to Sam's health. For now Sam was safe. Hopefully he'd recover enough until she came back for him. She could buy him a bit more time until she found a way to escape.

"I need my bag," she said finally. "And know this, mister, if you don't keep your word by letting us go once you have the urn, I will kill you with my bare hands."

The man let out a callous laugh.

"Oh, Miss Hunt, you crack me up! I have been chasing relics all around the world longer than what you've been breathing oxygen and believe me, I have no intentions of getting caught, ever, not by you or the authorities."

And with that, he snapped his fingers again and Alex was dragged out of the warehouse and back into the black van.

CHAPTER FOURTEEN

S till nauseated by having witnessed the despicable torture Sam had to endure, Alex sat in the back of the van as it drove off. For the very first time, the man with the black eyes spoke.

"Where do we need to go?"

It surprised Alex that he had a strong Asian accent and his somewhat high-pitched voice didn't quite resemble his muscular exterior. Alex paused as she recalled the first part of the riddle.

Where the three kings sleep...

The urge to ignore the ninja's question surged through her veins. She recalled the desperate look in Sam's eyes. She was out of options. There was no use fighting it any further. She had to comply.

"Oudong Temple. We need to go to the three stupas."

The driver accelerated. Twenty minutes later they stopped and, to further emphasize their power over her, abruptly pulled Alex from the van.

As usual, the temple was flooded with tourists. Alex looked at her hands that were still tied. She looked a mess. Her clothes were dirty and her shirt stained with Sam's blood.

"I need to clean up first. Unless of course you want the tourists to see that I'm being held captive? Oh, and another thing, your ninja suits are kind of giving it away too. You might want to consider changing into something a bit more appropriate for the occasion."

The three ninja kidnappers stopped. It was evident that the one with the black eyes was in charge when the other two looked at him for their orders. She had backed them into a corner. Removing their masks would expose their identities. He shoved her back into the van and tossed her backpack and a bottle of water onto the floor next to her before shutting the door.

When Alex stepped out of the van five minutes later the three ninja's had removed their masks and changed their black shirts to more casual t-shirts. At the back of their necks, all three of them had the distinctive black scorpion tattoo. Without their uniforms it was the only thing uniting them. Although they were all three Asian, they looked remarkably different. The man with the black eyes appeared slightly older with a scanty beard and mustache. A large tattoo of a tiger covered his entire right arm, and a red dragon decorated the other. With his mask off, his black eyes looked less pronounced against his thin lips that naturally curled up into a smile, even though he wasn't smiling at all.

The other two appeared to be at least ten years his junior. Their faces were clean and youthful and their arms clear from any tattoos. Alex was aware that tiger tattoos were the markings of the champion ring fighters that dominated the martial arts fight clubs across Asia. The red dragon was usually awarded only to the sensei, which confirmed her suspicions that the black-eyed man was in fact in charge.

Aware that Alex was sizing them up, the sensei lifted his shirt to reveal his .45 semi-automatic pistol that was tucked in his waistband.

She slung her backpack over her shoulder and started walking toward the flight of steps. If she were to successfully escape today, she'd have to create the perfect opportunity to disappear into the crowds. Perhaps she could disunite the trio; divide and conquer, as it were.

"Is your boss not joining us? Leaving you to do his dirty work for him, is he?" She provoked.

They didn't comment. Instead, Alex felt a strong hand between her shoulders when the black-eyed man shoved her forward. He might have had a mouth that hinted on a smile, but this man was far from pleasant. Annoyed with herself she headed up the multitude of steps to the stupas against the hill.

Halfway up her abductor stopped her.

"What are we looking for?"

It was evident he didn't want them to be too integrated with the crowds and lose control of the situation.

Alex took a sip of water and answered him mockingly.

"I'll let you know when I know."

Her cocky answer didn't fly. The black-eyed man pulled his gun from his waist, grabbed her by the arm and shoved it in her ribcage.

"Just because my boss isn't here doesn't mean you can mess with me woman."

As if his grip on her arm and the gun in her side wasn't warning enough he spat on the floor next to her, proving just how little respect he had for her. In an instant, Alex's bravery dissipated into a ball of dread inside her body. They might need her alive, but she could think of a million things he could do to hurt her without having to kill her. He had proven his loyalty to his puppet master already. She yanked her arm out from under his grip and looked him square in the eyes.

"I wasn't messing with you. I don't know what we're looking for. The riddle said, *Where the sun's rays meet,* and as it stands, it could be anywhere. Problem is, it's in the middle of the day, and the sun's rays are everywhere. The clue could just as well mean at first light or at sunset. It's impossible to know what time of day the sun is expected to hit at the exact point we're meant to be."

She stormed off up the stairs aware of him right behind her. This brute might have thought he had the upper hand, but she would not allow him to intimidate her. She needed to remain sharp and focused on getting as close as possible to the urn and grabbing the first opportunity to escape. She told the truth. There was no way of knowing what to look for. Once at the top, she would have a bird's eye view of the surrounds, and with any luck, she would spot something that revealed which direction to take.

As her emotions ran rampant with a jumble of fear and excitement she mulled the next part of the clue in her head.

The guardian of the ancient world sits at their feet

To her knowledge, both Greece and Rome had always referred to themselves as the ancient worlds, but in fact, the Chinese regarded themselves as having had the longest continuous civilization in the world. In all probability, the Chinese capital had been the most powerful economic center in the ancient world, attracting western traders to buy and sell silk by the multitudes. It made perfect sense that the clue referred to the 'ancient world' being China.

Alex knew they would soon reach the top of the fourth stupa, which would still be taped off and guarded. Based off of her recent visit granting her access using the Commissioner-General's letter, the guards on duty might not hesitate to let her pass. It was very likely that Roshi might be preparing the temple already. She couldn't endanger anyone else's life, least of all the monks'. Once they reached the row of three stupas halfway up the stairs, she stopped and pushed her way through the photo-snapping tourists to the eastern railing. Her entourage remained close on her heels and masterfully managed to avoid being photographed. From up high the view was as breathtaking as she recalled when she and Sam were there. Thousands of trees spread their foliage like umbrellas over the expansive hills below. Her eyes frantically searched the jungle for anything that could resemble 'the guardian of the world' but noticed nothing. The intense sun cast rays of light everywhere.

"What are we waiting for?" The man with the black eyes asked quietly. "Hurry up, my boss is not a patient man."

"I told you. I don't have the foggiest idea what we're looking for. I'm trying to find something called 'the guardian of the ancient world'. It has to be something that's of Chinese origin."

She recognized the path where they followed Roshi toward the secret tunnel but quickly diverted the ninja's attention by walking to the opposite side of the stupa. The secret tunnel could be her escape route if she managed to get away from them long enough without compromising the safety of the monks inside.

The three kidnappers flanked her like bodyguards around a celebrity, never once letting her out of their sight.

"There's nothing here. I told your boss. We need the second scroll. We're trying to find a needle in a haystack here."

She stalled, trying to buy Sam extra time to recover before she went back for him. She purposefully left out the 'sits at their feet' part of the clue. She had already figured out that the 'guardian of the ancient world' was the giant statue of Buddha behind her, but she dared not reveal it just yet. Her father always said deciphering clues was her strength. Somehow her mind connected the dots before anyone else could.

She walked along the railing that wrapped around the three stupas all the while pretending to still be scouting. By now it was late afternoon and as far as her kidnappers were concerned, nowhere close to finding the urn. She sensed they were becoming more agitated by the minute but she had an advantage which she had all intentions of exploiting for as long as possible. Sam needed to sufficiently build up his strength if they were to escape this unscathed.

Gradually the busloads of tourists departed one by one as night fell.

"We're going to have to sleep over tonight. I guess the clue will be revealed at first light when the sun's rays point it out. At least that's what I make of the clue."

Alex didn't wait for them to agree and headed down the steps back toward the van.

The night was not a peaceful one. Alex found her every move being watched. With her locked up in the back of the van, the kidnappers took shifts patrolling the bus throughout the night. At four a.m. the monks' morning bell chimed ever so faintly through the crisp morning air. Sunrise would be around five thirty. If her hunch was correct, the sun's rays would fall on the enormous Buddha in front of the three stupas.

She listened for the rustling sounds of the guards' feet outside but heard none. Was it possible they had fallen asleep? Surely men of such discipline would be alert at all times. She pushed open the door to see the youngest of the three kidnappers had indeed fallen asleep under a nearby tree. Alex froze as she spotted him and listened out for the other two who were nowhere to be seen. This might be her chance to escape to the tunnel. She should reach the path within five minutes and then it would be clear running to the hidden entrance. Without thinking about it further, she set off along the path.

Pain ripped through her right ankle moments before she hit the ground face first. Wrapped around her ankle was a black leather strap from a whip followed straightaway by the sensei's firm grip on her arm.

"What the heck?" She shouted at him in anger, irritated for having been caught.

"Where do you think you're going?" He replied.

The threat of his wrath engulfed her empty stomach.

"Nowhere, I needed the loo, or am I not permitted to urinate in private?" Alex yanked her arm from his grip.

"Go here." He pointed to the nearby tree and turned his back.

Unable to avoid it, she pretended to go behind the tree.

"We need to hurry. The sun will be up soon," she commanded as she charged past him toward the stupas' stairs. Her first attempt at escaping had failed miserably. Now, she would have to regain her focus and wait for the next opportunity.

A s predicted, the gigantic Buddha statue in front of the three stupas lit up like a cosmic nugget of gold just as the sun's first rays poured down from the skies. A shimmering beacon of light illuminated the glass box that was positioned at its feet. There was nothing inside the box but a small gold dish with old coins. Perplexed, Alex circled the statue.

"Where is it?" The sensei asked with more accusation than curiosity in his voice.

"I don't understand," Alex replied scratching her head. "It was supposed to show me."

The trio around her looked as confused as she did. She was confident something was meant to have happened at the Buddha's feet. But, apart from the box with coins, there was nothing there.

She stood back and stared at the Buddha. A minute later a beam of sunlight shone through the Buddha's forefinger and thumb and scattered a prism rainbow through the glass box onto the forest floor.

The magnitude and surpassing awe of the rainbow beam was so intense it beamed right across the entire balcony in front of the stupa and through the arches on top of the railing. It was simply spectacular. In that moment, Alex forgot all about her and Sam's capture. Instead, excitement leaped through her body as a force of adrenaline rushed her to the balcony's edge.

"The sun's rays! Where the sun's rays meet. The thumb and index finger is the traditional teaching pose!"

Without hesitation, she spun around and ran down the avalanche of steps into the forest. Her body thrust forward by the sheer excitement of the chase. She no longer schemed an escape even though there was a considerable distance between herself and her kidnappers behind her. All she thought of was to get to the end of the rainbow before the sun moved out of its position. She ran with the swiftness of a gazelle crisscrossing between the trees, never once taking her eyes off the intense beam of colors.

. . .

Out of breath she arrived at a small clearing surrounded by seven towering trees. Their leaves formed a dense canopy above her head that made way for the arch of colors at precisely the right angle. The precision and engineering with which the trees were positioned were astounding. Still panting she scoured the jungle floor underneath the prism beam. There was nothing but leaves scattered all over the ground. She vigorously brushed away the foliage with her hands. Her fingers hit the hard edges of something below the surface. She yanked her backpack off her back and took out her small shovel. Within minutes the steel grey coloring of a stone tablet stared back at her just as the colorful arch disappeared again between the leafy ceiling.

Before she even had a chance to properly inspect the ancient object, she was yanked back by the two younger gang members leaving the sensei to kneel down in front of the tablet. A quick phone call to his boss forced Alex back to the reality of a treasure hunt under duress. The mobile phone disappeared back into his pocket as he walked over to Alex and briefly instructed his two sidekicks to clear off the rest of the stone.

"Be careful!" Alex yelled remembering the warning of the puzzle.

"Shut up!" The black-eyed man shouted back, his eyes darker than usual.

Alex did as she was instructed. The warning in the clue echoed through her thoughts. *Beware the serpent's tongue! It is a trap.* She watched patiently as the two youths raked away more leaves. The stone, almost fully exposed now, was that of a dragon spanning at a minimum, eight meters in length. His face looked almost life-like as its scaled body stretched out between the roots of the trees. From its mouth, his forked tongue flicked upwards. Mesmerized, Alex watched as they excavated the stone serpent.

The sensei yelled another command to his men who promptly obeyed and started prodding and padding down the dragon's body. They shouted back an answer before both knelt over the tongue of the dragon which was the only part of its body protruding from the stone.

"No!" Alex shouted off a warning that brought about a firmer grip on her arm. It was blatantly obvious they thought she was attempting to deter them from unlocking the next clue.

"You're hurting me! Let go of my arm! You can't touch the tongue!" She tried warning them again.

Still, the men ignored her and continued prodding the stone tongue. In a wink of an eye, a loud swooshing sound swept through the air. Alex fell to the ground and covered her head pulling her clinging kidnapper down with her. The sound of two balls bouncing on the ground followed by two louder thuds forced Alex and the black-eyed man to look up. The gruesome sight of his decapitated subordinates lying on the ground left Alex and her kidnapper horrified.

When mobility finally returned to Alex's paralyzed limbs, she got up and cautiously walked over to the slain bodies next to the stone dragon. An enormous guillotine had ejected itself from the mantel on the dragon's neck.

The horrendous incident had little to no effect on the black-eyed man's demeanor. He showed no remorse or emotion of any kind and merely pulled the dismembered corpses and remains under a nearby tree. With his hands on his hips, he then towered over Alex and barked a command at her to carry on.

His frigid behavior somewhat surprised her. Could these men have this little value for another member of their gang's life? She didn't care for them either, but if ever she became more aware of how brutal and callus her kidnappers were, it was then.

Resolving to comply with her abductor's demands, she recalled the next part of the clue.

Steer clear and follow the map.

"We're looking for a map of some kind," she offered. "Something that will show us where to go next."

They leaned over the dragon and inspected the carvings. The man searched fervently alongside her. At that moment, she missed Sam dearly and wondered if he had survived the torture.

"Here!" Her hostile associate shouted excitedly as he pointed to the imprints on the dragon's tail.

Alex noticed the map carved out in the stone. It would lead them through the forest, and she quickly copied it down on her notepad. Closer inspection delivered several routes in the map. She turned it upside down, folded the paper's corners together and still couldn't quite ascertain which direction they needed to follow.

"Fire!" She shouted excitedly. "The clue says 'the fire is your ally, it will light the way'."

She sat back down next to the dragon's tail and traced her finger along the lines before digging into her backpack for a packet of matches.

The first match onto the dragon's tail had no effect. She struck the second match at the tip of the serpent's tail. Within seconds sparks flew through the air as it lit up the distinct outlines of the route they should take. From under his breath, the black-eyed man rambled off something in Mandarin, which made her smile. It was apparent he had never seen anything like it.

After briefly copying the map onto her notebook they were set. Alex stared at the diagram. There was one last clue left.

Keep to the center until you reach the clay

Two of the men were dead. She stood a far better chance of escaping now, but she'd have to stall. Once they reached the 'clay'—whatever that meant—they would not be able to continue without the second scroll's clues. Since she tried to warn them against the peril of the serpent's tongue, he trusted her. The black-eyed man would be none the wiser now that he had tasted the rush from an archaeological treasure hunt.

So, for the most part of the day, Alex pretended to follow the map leading them deep into the forest. It was afternoon, and they were several hours' walk from the Oudong Temple where the van was parked. Alex sat down on the root of a large tree.

"I'm tired, I don't think the map is accurate," she lied.

"Get up!" the man barked. "We will go back to the van."

He stared at his mobile and raised it above his head. He had missed his hourly check-in with his boss. The black-eyed man was exactly where Alex wanted him. She jumped up and headed back the way they came. Once they were nearing the van, she stopped.

"I need to use the bathroom. Turn around."

This was her moment. The black-eyed man politely turned his back and continued searching for the mobile's reception. Alex picked up the fair sized rock she had spotted earlier and whacked him on the back of his head. It wasn't hard enough to knock him out, and he merely swayed. She struck his head again, and this time the brawny black-eyed man slumped to the ground. Alex wasn't sure if she had killed him, her conscious instantly plaguing her. Blood gushed from the second wound to his head. She kicked his side for any sign of life, but there was none. He was indeed dead. Tears of horror threatened to run down her face but she quickly wiped it away and thrust her hands in his pockets in search of the car keys. She never intended to kill him, but if she hadn't, it was a matter of time before he killed her. With the keys in hand she bolted for the car as fast as her legs could carry her.

CHAPTER FIFTEEN

With her foot flat on the accelerator, Alex sped back onto the byway toward the city. Trusting only her memory and senses, she looked at her wristwatch. When the kidnappers left the warehouse with her earlier that morning, it was roughly twenty minutes to the Oudong temple. She reduced her pace to what she estimated their speed was.

Her eyes frantically searched for a road that was meant to turn off the road. Recalling the name from the faded sign at the abandoned warehouses, she looked for any pointer signs, but there were none. She pulled the van over to the side of the road. It had to be close. The minibus motored slowly down the road. Up ahead Alex spotted an overgrown dirt road and decided to take a chance at it. The bumpy road brought about some familiarity, but she couldn't be sure. It was then she became aware of the tall steel pipes from the deserted factory plant next to the warehousing. Her heart leaped out through her throat. This was it! She had found Sam's location. If only she knew how to get him out.

She reduced the van's speed to a quiet murmur as she rolled closer. If guards were watching the entrance she'd be detected, so she veered off the dirt road and parked under a nearby tree. Hunched over she used the van to hide behind and scouted across at the deserted industrial plant. It was ghostly quiet. The luxury black sedan was no longer parked out front, and there were no signs of any life. She was positive this was the right place but nevertheless searched for the faded name sign. Relieved, she spotted it much further up along the fence.

Sam's warehouse was about a hundred and sixty feet ahead of her. She was sure there would be at least two guards patrolling the perimeter, but she couldn't see anyone. Doubt entered her mind over the possibility that they might have moved Sam. She needed to be sure though and there was no way of knowing without going in.

She'd have to take her chances and make a clear run for it. She couldn't risk getting captured now. Apprehension gripped her throat and her pulse throbbed at her temples. It's now or never. Scanning the perimeter she set off toward the boundary posts. Her legs felt heavy as she sprinted across the thick terrain. Once at the fence, she fell flat onto the ground between the bushes praying no one saw here. She paused and surveyed the area again. Still, there was no sight of anyone. Crawling on her elbows, she reached the entrance gate, which was padlocked from the inside. Not much of a climber she resolved that she would have to squeeze through the gap. Alex wedged her body between the two gateposts. Frazzled by the rattling sound of the heavy chain and padlock against the fence, she bolted across the tarmac and ducked behind the nearby water tanks. Gasping for air, she decided to stay put to make sure she wasn't heard or seen.

Several minutes later and everything was still as quiet as when she had arrived. Her eyes were glued to the warehouse door. Having regained her breath, she readied herself for another quick run to the warehouse. The crackling sound of tires on a dirt road alarmed her. Two cars pulled up to the entrance gate behind her, and she crouched back behind the water tanks. Alex watched as two luxury black cars drove through the gates and parked a mere thirty feet in front of her. An Asian chauffeur climbed out of the front car and opened the rear door for another male to step out. He was not Asian and impeccably dressed from head to toe in a black pinstriped suit. His raven hair was tied back into a low ponytail. Beneath it, the tail of a black scorpion tattoo was visible just above his white collar.

Alex held her breath praying for them not to see her. She dared not make a sound. She was too close. Sweat trickled down the outer corner of her brow. Still hunched, her legs quivered uncontrollably. Alarmed by the possibility that the top of her head might be showing she fell on her hands and knees in a crawling position and peered around the containers.

From the second black car another three male figures appeared who walked over to the man in the black suit. What Alex saw next knocked her wind out. Her eyes didn't deceive her. There was no mistaking one of the three men's identities. It was Ollie, a very formal looking Ollie dressed in black pants and a white collared shirt. Alex blinked several times. It looked nothing like the bantering Aussie from the Australian outback she had met before. Alex poked her head further out from behind the tank to see better. She watched as Ollie shook hands with the man in the suit whose authoritative voice cut across the barren industrial site. Alex shut her eyes as she recognized his voice. He was her kidnapper. The man she never saw, the man who ordered Sam's torture with the snapping of his fingers, the ringleader.

A wave of nausea engulfed her insides. She always knew there was something off with Ollie. Her instincts had been substantiated. He was one of them. Alex crawled back behind the water tanks and listened to the men exchange pleasantries. She wasn't sure whether she wanted to cry or rush over and knock their lights out. Fighting the urge to be the GI Jane in her head, Alex bit down hard on her lip. Sam was still in there, and she couldn't leave there without him. No, she had to get a hold of herself and wait for the right moment to make her next move.

Relieved that the water tanks provided sufficient hiding, she sneaked another look at the group of men. Ollie had his back toward her and there, in the nape of his neck, the image of a black scorpion stared back at her. Alex cursed under her breath. Vile visions of punching his lights out plagued her thoughts. She should have known. This betraying fraudster knew their every move. He had been ahead of them all this time, and they walked right into his trap. Alex wiped the sweat from her right eye as she listened in on their conversation. They were talking about the urn and relishing in the knowledge that, as far as they knew, Alex was out with their men finding it.

That made Alex smile with satisfaction. These corrupt criminals had no idea that at least two of their gang members were dead and that she had managed to escape. She was ahead in their wicked little game of chess. Several minutes later the men, including Ollie, got back into their cars and left the site as quickly as they had arrived. This must have been their rendezvous point. To Alex's surprise there were still no guards anywhere near the warehouse. Alex waited a few more minutes just to be sure they were gone and ran to the warehouse door. It was locked from the outside with another padlock. She cursed their attention to detail and looked around for something that could break the door open. A rusted metal pole the size of a crowbar lay around the side of the warehouse. She had never needed to break open a lock, but she had seen similar scenes in the movies. It couldn't be that hard, she thought and pounced on the padlock. Within seconds the inferior latch popped off the door and the chain fell with a loud clanging to the floor. If there were in fact any guards inside or nearby, they would be sure to come running, so she gripped the make-shift crowbar and lay back against the warehouse wall behind the open door. She was in luck. No one came.

Alex slipped inside the dark storeroom. The beam of sunlight shone a torchlight through the pitch-black depot. It was completely empty. Gripping the steel rod, she stealthily moved across to the staircase and briefly paused. The rusty steel steps groaned under her feet as she cautiously climbed them. At the top of the stairs, the door was closed. Her knuckles were white as she clasped the steel pipe firmer and yanked the door open.

Sam lay on a dirty mattress in the corner of the small room. His hands and feet were tied.

"Sam!" A relieved Alex cried out and rushed to his side. "Are you alone?" she added as she untied the ropes.

The smile on Sam's swollen face melted her heart.

"You're a sight for sore eyes, Alex Hunt," Sam replied wearily. "I knew you'd come for me."

"Of course I would, silly. Are you okay? Can you walk?"

Sam merely nodded. He was still quite weak and had several cracked ribs.

"We need to get out of here, we don't have much time," Alex added as she helped him up and swung his arm over her shoulders.

Sam groaned under the pain in his ribs as they descended the stairs. They had barely reached the bottom when they spotted two ninja guards running through the open warehouse door. Grateful for the poorly lit room, they huddled under the stairs sending stabs of pain through Sam's tortured body.

"Shh!" Alex whispered covering his mouth with her hand.

The guards ran up the stairs above them and, within seconds, came storming back down. Barking commands at each other they searched frantically for their escaped prisoner before they left the warehouse and ran back outside.

"Now what?" Sam whispered.

Alex paused as she tried to come up with their next move.

"Can you run?"

"That depends. How fast and how far?"

"I have a van parked about a hundred and sixty feet on the other side of the fence. Wait here."

Alex glided against the wall toward the open warehouse door and popped her head outside to gauge the guards' locations. They had split up and were hysterically running between the storerooms in search of their escapee. She ran back and pulled Sam from underneath the staircase.

"Let's go!"

Hunched over Sam obeyed.

"See those tanks over there? We need to bolt for them. Think you can make it?"

"Do I have a choice?" Sam smiled.

When the coast was clear the pair ran from the warehouse and ducked behind the tanks just in time before spotting the two guards run back inside the warehouse. Without a second thought Alex ran back to the warehouse and slammed the door shut behind them. She ran the chain around the handles and wedged the steel rod through the links.

"That should buy us some time," she announced as she helped Sam up and ushered him to the gate entrance.

The opening between the gates was too narrow for Sam to get through and having used the steel pipe to lock the guards inside the warehouse, Alex was out of options. She frantically looked around in search of a solution.

"Wait here," she ordered and hurriedly slipped through the gate.

A minute later Sam watched as Alex came speeding down the dirt road toward the gate, managing to take cover just in time before she blasted through the gates with the minibus.

"Get in!" She rushed Sam along as she flung the passenger door open from the inside.

Once inside the van, a stunned Sam looked across at her as she powered up the dirt road toward the highway.

"Okay, who are you and what have you done with Alex?"

Still wide-eyed with adrenaline rushing through her veins, Alex broke into laughter. "I missed you, Sam Quinn."

Sam smiled wincing with pain as the minivan hit a significant bump in the road. "Now what?"

Alex paused. His question reminded her that they were on the run.

"I have no idea, Sam. But we're not safe anywhere. Ollie is a scorpion guy too."

With still swollen eyes, Sam looked sideways at Alex. This wasn't her usual suspicious intuition talking. She was dead serious.

"You're joking, right?"

"I'm afraid not. I saw the traitor with my very own eyes, outside the warehouse. I hid behind the water tanks and he and the perfect English-speaking kidnapper pulled up in fancy black cars. They were very friendly with each other. They both had scorpion tattoos on the back of their necks. Just like the bikers, and he wasn't in his Aussie safari clothes either. The guy was neatly dressed up in black pants and a crisp, white shirt, like someone important."

The pair went quiet as they reached the end of the dirt road.

"Which way? Left or right?" Alex asked. Without waiting for a still surprised Sam to answer she turned left toward the town.

"We need to go to Mr. Yeng-Pho and report all we know. He's the only one that can help us now."

The engine picked up speed as they pushed toward the Commissioner-General's office building.

. . .

T he revolving doors posed a challenge when Alex helped Sam walk into the Cambodian judicial department. Assuming Alex and Sam were a threat, the paramilitary guards took one look at Sam's tortured body and pulled their weapons.

"No, no! We're here to see Mr. Yeng-Pho. We were kidnapped. He knows us!" Alex explained causing more of a commotion than intended.

Moments later two more guards joined them, and before you knew it, the department was up in arms.

"Please? Just call Mr. Yeng-Pho. Tell him Alex Hunt and Sam Quinn are here. We need his help!"

Still suspicious, one of the guards radioed someone, and several minutes later, Mr. Yeng-Pho came to their rescue.

"Miss Hunt?" He yelled surprised, ordering his men to let them go.

"Mr. Yeng-Pho! Oh thank heavens. They kidnapped us, and Sam is hurt. You have to help us!" Alex cried out.

Still caught off guard by the pair's surprise arrival, Mr. Yeng-Pho ushered them into a closed office and ordered his men to stand down and leave the room.

Alone in the room, the Commissioner-General sat them down. "Miss Hunt, please continue. Who kidnapped you? Tell me everything you know."

F or the next hour, Alex described the entire ordeal in great detail. How they met Ollie and their stay at his hideout in the middle of the jungle. How they discovered the scroll that led them to Vietnam. About how Sam got shot, their kidnapping and his torture.

"Miss Hunt, this was a most unfortunate event, but please tell me, are you saying there is in fact another golden urn and that the one that got stolen was a counterfeit?"

Alex nodded. "Exactly! One the Royal family was aware of, in fact. Apparently, it is protocol for them to hide the original one, to protect it from ever being stolen."

Mr. Yeng-Pho leaned forward. "And you have the authentic urn in your possession?"

"Not quite, no but I'm certain I can find it. The scorpion men blackmailed me to find it. With the clues from the first scroll I have managed to already complete half the search but since they held Sam captive, I had to escape and go back for him and now we're here."

Mr. Yeng-Pho pulled out his chair and clasped his hands together. "Please excuse me for a moment. I'll be right back."

Alone in the closed office, Alex breathed a big sigh of relief for the first time in days. Sam sat quietly next to her, still holding his ribs.

"It's going to be okay, Sam. We're going to get you medical attention and put all of this behind us. Hang in there, okay?"

"Nothing a good plate of food won't fix. The bruising will subside and I don't suspect my ribs to be broken. I'll be fine in a couple of days," Sam replied.

The two sat silently waiting for Mr. Yeng-Pho to return.

Sam tapped his fingers on the table. "Where do you think Mr. Yeng-Pho went? He didn't say much did he?"

As if the Commissioner-General was right outside listening at the door, he re-entered the office.

"Please come with me," pulling out Alex's chair.

Without a moment's hesitation, Alex helped Sam up and followed Mr. Yeng-Pho into the parking garage in the basement. A scrawny looking Asian man accompanied them and ushered them toward a parked black sedan. Alex paused as they neared the vehicle. Her pulse raced as she realized what was going down. Seconds later Mr. Yeng-Pho pulled a gun from his jacket's breast pocket and pointed it at them.

"You didn't honestly think you'd get away with this, did you?" he sneered. "Get in!" pointing to the car.

His scrawny sidekick produced his own weapon and shoved it in Sam's bruised side.

Confusion lay bare across Alex and Sam's faces.

"You're one of them?" A still in shock Alex asked after which Mr. Yeng-Pho exploded in a mocking laugh.

"ONE of them? Miss Hunt, you underestimate me. I'm THE one! I'm in charge of this entire operation. Now get in before I shoot the charming Dr. Quinn and put him out of his misery."

Mr. Yeng-Pho's scrawny sidekick shoved Alex and Sam into the backseat of the car, cuffed their hands to the door handles and taped their mouths shut. The Commissioner-General slipped in the front seat and instructed his accomplice to drive.

Alex felt utterly broken and defeated as she looked across at Sam who showed much the same evidence of betrayal on his face. How did they get this so terribly wrong?

Handcuffed to the car, and unable to speak, tears flooded Alex's eyes. Fear ripped through her body while feelings of total hopelessness overwhelmed her. Her heart felt heavy with the prospect of not knowing where they were going and how they were going to escape or survive this awful turn of events.

CHAPTER SIXTEEN

The two decapitated bodies lay waiting for them under the tree when Alex, Sam, and their new kidnapper arrived at the stone dragon site. The black-eyed man was nowhere to be seen. If he survived the blow to his head, he would have somehow made his way back to his gang.

The barefoot walk into the jungle left Sam exhausted. Struggling to breathe under the immense pain of his cracked ribs he somehow managed to keep up. Alex was thrilled she had the foresight to put the treasure map in her pants' pocket when they searched her backpack and subsequently found nothing. Mr. Yeng-Pho's gun held them captive while his scrawny accomplice took great pleasure in shoving them around.

"Where is it?" Mr. Yeng-Pho barked. "There's no escaping this, Miss Hunt so unless you want your friend here to die, you'll tell me where the urn is."

His scrawny partner ripped the silver tape off her mouth leaving behind a stinging red patch around her mouth. Alex knew his sadistic action was done with intent to entice a reaction from her, so she clenched her jaw and fought the urge to spit in his face. He stared directly at her when he yanked Sam's tape off his mouth. Alex still didn't give him the satisfaction of reacting. Instead, Sam sneakily pushed his leg forward. The scrawny bastard tripped and fell face first into a pile of leaves. Though Sam's face professed no blame, it nevertheless earned him a backhand slap across the face.

"So if we're done playing, I'm waiting," Mr. Yeng-Pho remarked while giving his colleague a stern look.

"I don't have it. I told you already. This was as far as we got," Alex lied.

Mr. Yeng-Pho didn't answer immediately and paced around the dragon before stopping behind Alex. With his mouth close to her ear and his fingers twirling a strand of her hair, he whispered.

"Stop fighting, Miss Hunt."

His hand gripped her hair and yanked her head back firmly.

"Don't make me get it out of you the hard way. I'm sure your esteemed colleague will vouch how little he enjoyed being tortured."

The commissioner shoved her head forward causing her to lose her balance and fall to her knees in front of the dragon.

"Give it to him, Alex. It's not worth it!" Sam spoke.

"I'd listen to him, Miss Hunt. Where is the urn?"

Sam was right. It wasn't worth being killed over. She would play along and find another way of escaping.

"There's a map. It's in my back pocket." She took the map from her pants pocket and turned around for Yeng-Pho to take it from her bound hands.

The assistant snatched it and delivered it to Mr. Yeng-Pho.

"Great, now we're getting somewhere. Lead the way, Miss Hunt," planting his flat hand on her back to shove her forward.

The map led them on an hour trail of counting paces and changing direction through the overgrown Cambodian hills behind the Oudong Temple. The blazing sun was hot and uncomfortable. With their hands still tied behind their backs, blades of tall grass cut their faces as Alex and Sam fought through the rough terrain.

Alex stopped and looked back at their kidnappers behind them. "Can you at least untie our hands so we can get through in one piece?" she begged. "And we need water. We haven't had anything in days."

The humidity had taken its toll on Mr. Yeng-Pho too who had his uniform jacket tied around his waist, and his sleeves rolled up.

"Fine, but know this, Miss Hunt. If either of you decide to run, I'll kill you on the spot. Is that clear?" Cocking his gun and pointing it at her face.

Alex nodded in agreement. According to the map, their destination should be very close; thirty paces southwest followed by sixty paces north.

Shortly after, they arrived at what the scroll referred to as 'the clay.' Expecting to see a significant clay pot or statue of some kind, to all of their surprises, it was a pool of quicksand spanning roughly sixteen feet in diameter.

"This is it," Alex said apprehensively. "This is where the map and the first scroll's riddle end."

"So the clay refers to a large puddle of quicksand," Sam said matter-of-factly as he sat down under a shading tree. "Now what?"

"I don't know. Honorable Commissioner, now what? There's no telling whereto from here without the second scroll." Alex plonked herself down next to Sam.

Mr. Yeng-Pho wiped his brow and squatted in front of the pair.

"Again you underestimate me. Do you honestly think I would be out here in the blazing sun if I didn't know what I was doing?"

He pulled a piece of paper from his jacket pocket and tossed it into Alex's lap before cocking his gun in her face again.

"Crack it, Miss famous archaeologist," he added. "We don't have all day."

Alex unfolded the paper. It was a copy of the second scroll.

"Where did you get this?" She exclaimed jumping to her feet. "I was told it burned in the fire during the Khmer Rouge attacks."

"Clearly it hadn't," Sam commented. "Who are you really, Mr. Yeng-Pho?"

"Well, look at you? Aren't you the clever one?" the commissioner answered sarcastically.

"As it happens, Dr. Quinn, my uncle was responsible for the fire that day, but thanks to his immense wisdom, he salvaged the scroll before it could be destroyed." Mr. Yeng-Pho turned and gripped Alex by the arm. "Now, get on with it! Crack the next riddle and find me that urn!"

"Why is this golden urn so important to you? As far as I know, it contains the Buddha's body parts and should have no value to you. Unless you want to tell me that you're actually a monk and need to ask for forgiveness," Alex mocked.

The scrawny sidekick slapped Alex hard across the face. This time, Alex didn't hold back and flung a ball of saliva into his face before thrusting her small fist across his cheekbone. Instantly the guy reacted by pinning Alex against the tree and shoving his gun under her chin.

Mr. Yeng-Pho barked a stern warning and gripped his associate by the throat to stand down. Begrudgingly he obeyed and wiped the spit from his face.

"I said, decode the clues and let's get on with it!"

Alex smoothed out the now crumpled piece of paper and read it out loud.

Weight is your foe, so find its right place

> For the moon to cast its shadow
> And help you find the face
> Watch out for the evil eye that points to the sky
> Your goal is to bend low for the truth to bestow

"Now that's a conundrum if ever you've seen one," Sam commented.

Alex didn't say a word. In silence, she read the clue several times again.

"Well, don't just stand there. What are we dealing with here?" An annoyed Mr. Yeng-Pho nudged.

The small group watched impatiently as Alex paced up and down along the quicksand pool, pausing in front of Sam.

"How much do you weigh?"

"Weigh? I have no idea."

Mr. Yeng-Pho stepped up next to her. "What does that have to do with anything?"

Alex turned to face him. "Everything in fact. The first line reads, 'weight is your foe, so find the right place.'"

"Yes, and?" The Commissioner-General snapped back.

"And...the clay is quicksand," Alex explained.

"Indeed!" Sam chipped in excitedly. "The heavier you are in quicksand, the more you agitate the composition. It's your enemy."

Alex smiled proudly at Sam for getting it.

"Exactly, so in the case of the 'clay,' weight is your enemy, but, if you 'find the right place,' somehow the moon will cast a shadow and reveal some sort of a face."

"Well, I'm certainly the heaviest," said Sam. "So let's find the right place."

"What exactly are we looking for?" Mr. Yeng-Pho asked, it could be anything."

"Anything, except the quicksand, that is," Sam said with irony in his voice.

For the next forty-five minutes, the party scoured the surrounds for anything that might fit the bill.

"I think I found it!" Sam shouted beckoning for Alex to join him.

He had been searching between the leaves in a tree and noticed an odd-looking branch protruding from the tree.

"It seems to be some sort of a lever," Sam added.

"I'd agree. Let's hope it's not booby-trapped. You okay to do this Sam?"

"Never been better."

Sam placed both hands on the fake branch slightly above his head. The thought of having to hang much in the same way he did in the warehouse twisted his insides in a knot. Sensing his thoughts, Alex flashed him an encouraging smile. It was their only option if they were to complete their mission and get out of this alive. Sam's bruised muscles and cracked ribs labored his breathing. He stretched up and pulled the lever down with the full force of his weight. A loud rumbling sound echoed from beyond the pool of quicksand as they felt the ground shake beneath their feet.

As the loose wet sand slowly gave way, an upright structure ascended. In the middle of the murky pool, the shape of a stone spear pushed out of the quicksand and towered above the group who stood in awe.

When the ground eventually stopped trembling under their feet, Alex and Sam slowly moved toward the spear. Roughly the height of a two-story building, and with all the mud cleared away, it was a majestic sight. Hundreds of red, yellow and green gemstones sparkled prisms of colorful light as the last of the sun's intense rays fell on it.

There was no way of getting to the spear for as quickly as the slushy sand gave way, it closed up around its base again. It stood tall in its entire luring splendor.

"What's next?" Yeng-Pho said impatiently.

"We wait," Sam said to which Alex agreed and added, "Exactly, we need to wait 'for the moon to cast its shadow' and help us find the face."

Yeng-Pho looked up at the sun. "It will be dark in a couple of hours. We'll stay here."

Several hours later, when the moon finally sat high enough to shine through the tall trees, Sam woke Alex up who had fallen asleep against him.

"It's time Alex. Look," Sam whispered.

Jumping to their feet, they all watched as the moonlight beamed down on the jeweled spear that sparkled like a million stars all around them. The brightest of sapphire blue light glowed from the tip of the spear and projected across the mud pool.

"Come! Hurry!" Alex shouted as she led them around the pool to where the blue light radiated onto a group of trees. It was a spectacular festival of lights culminating into this one spot between the lush green leaves. And there, as if watching in slow motion, the vines made way for an ancient face carved from stone.

Alex grabbed onto Sam's arm in awe of what transpired in front of them.

"I bet this is where it gets interesting," Sam whispered to Alex.

She squeezed Sam's arm with excitement.

When the face was fully visible, Yeng-Pho pushed Alex and Sam out of the way.

"What's the next clue?" He urged.

"You might not want to get too close Yeng-Pho. It says to watch out for the evil eye that points to the sky," Alex cautioned.

They stood back to inspect the face.

"Which is it though? One is looking at us, and the other seems to not exist. Or is it closed?" Sam asked perplexed.

Alex pulled the now crumpled paper from her pocket and started pacing back and forth. Her eyes scanned over the clue.

"And?" Yeng-Pho prompted for her to read it out loud.

"'The goal is to bend low for the truth to bestow'."

Alex tugged at Sam's arm as she bent low in front of the face. Expectantly they watched the face but nothing happened.

"This better not be one of your tricks, Miss Hunt. Why are you stalling?" Yeng—Pho warned her by pushing his gun in her back.

"I'm not! We just need to be patient," Alex told him off. "Trust me. If the clue warns you against something, then you had better believe it. Ask your two dead puppets back at the dragon. They didn't listen to me either."

Yeng-Pho cocked his pistol and stood back. "Well, I don't trust you, but you're both dead if you're lying to me."

Sam nudged with his elbow and pointed his chin at the stone face between the vines. The blue light that shone from the spear had turned to a ruby red as the moonlight hit another gemstone in the javelin behind them. The beam reflected onto the pupil of the open eye.

"Get down!" Alex shouted while her and Sam both fell to the ground.

A series of arrows shot in quick succession from the statued face's mouth, narrowly missing Yeng-Pho. Behind him, his partner in crime wasn't so lucky. A dozen arrows pierced his body as he fell dead to his knees.

The trio lay face down on the jungle floor until the flying arrows subsided. When Alex finally looked up, her heart skipped several beats when she caught sight of the opening below the ancient face.

"Do you see what I'm seeing?" an equally stunned Sam asked.

"Get up!" Yeng-Pho kicked their legs. "Move!"

With his gun pointed at Sam and Alex, he bullied them away from the opening. Satisfied they were a safe enough distance away from him, he bent down and pulled the golden urn from the small hidden cave between the vines. Staring down the barrel of Yeng-Pho's gun, Sam and Alex watched his surprised face turn into a smug grin. Distracted by his self-absorbed ego and greed, Yeng-Pho set the urn down on the ground.

"Eleven years!" Yeng-Pho cried out excitedly. "Eleven years I've waited for this moment and it's finally all mine!"

Drowned in pride and self-satisfaction, he lifted the lid off the gold urn and pulled out a gold amulet with a large ruby stone.

Alex gasped as she laid eyes on the dangling stone. Stunned by the unexpected find, she watched as he wrapped it around his fingers and held it up to the light. The ruby sparkled, casting rays of dark red light across the jungle floor.

"So that's what you've been after all along," Alex said forcing Yeng-Pho's attention back to them.

"This, my dear Miss Hunt, is worth a small fortune. It has been lost for more than two thousand years! But now I have it! I finally have it!"

He steadied his gun on them. "Now, if the two of you don't mind, I have some money to make. Money I'm not prepared to share with anyone."

Yeng-Pho waived his gun at them to get moving.

Ushered by his gun's barrel, Yeng-Pho forced Alex and Sam toward the quicksand.

"What fools you two are. Did you honestly think I would share this moment with anyone? Buddha's amulet is one of the biggest ancient treasures known to mankind. My buyers will kill over this, which brings me to the two of you. My identity has remained hidden for years and I'm certainly not intending on getting exposed now. This has to look like an accident, so it seems the two of you are going to take a little swim and allow the entire world to think the famous Alex Hunt and Sam Quinn died in action on an archaeological expedition. It's perfect! It couldn't have worked out more in my favor."

Sam took Alex's hand as they reached the edge of the quicksand and squeezed it tight. She didn't cry. Though inside her chest her heart was being crushed, she felt immense pride to have come this far on their expedition.

"This has been quite an adventure, Alex Hunt."

CHAPTER SEVENTEEN

Alex and Sam's parting moment was interrupted as Ollie's voice cut through the air behind them.

"What on earth...you traitor!" Alex yelled. She had nothing to lose now. If she were to die here today it might as well be after she told Ollie what a lowlife scumbag he was for deceiving them.

Ollie's hunting rifle had been replaced by a machine gun that casually hung over his shoulder. Yeng-Pho's audacious laughter was nauseating.

"Another surprise for you tonight Miss Hunt. My dear friend, Oliver is on my payroll, in charge of my infiltration team, in fact. I wouldn't have been able to do this without his inside track," he said proudly.

"No surprise there Yeng-Pho. I knew he was up to no good from the moment I lay eyes on him. You two suit each other. You're despicable," Alex spat at their feet to which Sam added,

"You were the last person on earth I thought capable of such loathsome acts, Ollie. How could you? You certainly pulled the Aussie wool over my eyes."

Yeng-Pho laughed out loud again, clutching the Buddha amulet in his greedy paws. "And thanks to him you're about to meet your maker Dr. Quinn."

He turned to Ollie, "Finish them off, Oliver. There's money to be made."

Ollie swung his firearm from his shoulder and aimed it at Alex and Sam.

Alex didn't have any fight left in her. This was it. Tears ran down her cheeks as she drew in a deep shuddering breath. Her chest felt heavy under the weight of betrayal and knowing it was the last time she'd ever hunt a treasure with Sam hurt like crazy. This is not how she wanted to die. Staring down the barrel of Ollie's weapon, her body shook uncontrollably as Sam pulled her into his arms.

"You heard the man, Sheila. The night is full of surprises." Ollie said as he turned his rifle away from Alex and Sam and aimed it at the Commissioner-General. "I think the time has finally come, Yeng-Pho. You're under arrest."

"FEDERAL POLICE! GET DOWN ON THE GROUND!"

Chaotic shouts by members of the armed forces ripped through the night air as they announced themselves. Sam pulled Alex to the ground and shielded her head. They watched the frenzy of red lasers and torchlights scatter everywhere as the police searched for more of Yeng-Pho's men. Within seconds they had him in handcuffs and pinned to the ground. A helicopter roared loudly above their heads sending gusts of wind and dirt in their faces. With seasoned precision, Yeng-Pho was hoisted up into the helicopter and flown away.

"What the heck is going on here?" Sam shouted at Ollie who was talking on a sat phone.

"It's all over, Mate. Operation Buddha was successful."

Ollie extended his arm to help Sam and Alex up. "We could have never done this without you, Sheila. Thank you."

"What are you talking about? Who are you and what's all this 'Operation Buddha' business?" Alex shouted at Ollie.

"Calm down, Sheila. Mission accomplished. Allow me to introduce myself. My name is Matt Taylor, Special Agent Matt Taylor from the Australian Security Intelligence Organization, ASIO in short."

"Matt? 'Special Agent'? What do you mean you're a special agent?" A gobsmacked Alex tried to make sense of it all.

"Don't look so surprised, Sheila. I'm not really the low-life you accused me of." Matt joked. "I'm one of the good guys. Operation Buddha was an undercover sting operation to flush out the head of the snake, or the tail of the scorpion, in actual fact. We've been after the Scorpions for years, and I've been undercover for the last five trying to catch this bastard in the act."

Sam scratched his head. "Ollie, Matt or whoever you are, I'm usually a clever bloke, but you're going to need to start at the beginning. We have no idea what you're talking about."

"It's Matt. Ollie is my cover name, and the two of you were instrumental in helping us. The Scorpions is an international underground syndicate who smuggles stolen artifacts and sells them on the black market for top dollar. FBI, MI5, and ASIO. the list goes on. We've all been tracking their corruption all over the world; always only catching the small guys, but we've never been able to find out who the mastermind behind the entire Scorpions syndicate was, until we followed Intel here to Cambodia. I went undercover to flush him out, and the golden urn was the perfect bait."

Alex still couldn't believe her ears. "So wait, where do Roshi and the monks fit in and how did you know about the amulet?"

"Ah Sheila I told you, the monks and I go way back. They were approached by ASIO to help me infiltrate and protect my cover. In return, I promised to find them the golden urn and return it to its rightful place. That's when they told me about Buddha's amulet. Quite a rare find, isn't it?" Matt stopped and looked the pair up and down, "You both look like you could do with some food, and something tells me you're not going to say no to my bear stew tonight, hey Sheila?"

T he Royal Palace was as majestic as it sounded. Waiting in the large foyer, two security personnel flanked Alex and Sam as they patiently waited for the king and Prime Minister to arrive. When they finally got ushered to a formal sitting room, Sam looked at Alex and said,

"Out of all our expeditions together, this one took the cake. I can't recall Professor Keating ever saying torture and flushing out international syndicates were part of the job description."

Alex admired one of the paintings on the wall.

"You're right. It's not in the job description, but it seems the world isn't quite what it used to be either. It certainly has been an adventure, hasn't it?" She smiled and turned to face him. " I'm just glad you're okay. I don't think I could have survived this without you."

Moments later a small party of security personnel entered the room followed by His Royal Majesty of Cambodia, the Prime Minister and none other than Roshi and the Great Senior Patriarch.

The king spoke in a gentle, warm voice as he stood before Sam and Alex.

"What an incredible honor to meet you both, Miss Hunt and Dr. Quinn. The Cambodian government owes you a great amount of gratitude for finding the Golden Urn, not to mention our venerable Buddha's amulet. To be honest, we all thought the amulet was a legend. But to find it here on Cambodian soil is the greatest gift, thank you."

The king paused and somberly turned to Sam.

"Dr. Quinn, please accept our sincere apologies for the despicable manner in which you were treated here in our beautiful country. We are most happy you are still alive, and if there is ever anything we can do to compensate for the horrible experience you've had, please let me know."

The Prime Minister went to stand next to him. "Miss Hunt, Dr. Quinn, we would very much like if you would both join us in the celebratory procession to the Temple. Would you care to accompany us, please?"

Alex looked across at the senior monk who smiled and nodded with approval. To be invited by the king and his royals to join them in such a big event was the most significant honor yet.

"But of course, your Highness. It would be our honor," Alex swiftly accepted.

Outside the palace the street was crowded with thousands of Cambodians as they waited for the king to lead the parade to the mountain shrine. Several citizens cheered as the king placed the golden urn in the float, which resembled a giant golden swan built around a small car. Four Buddhist monks sat praying on each of the corners of the float as the procession moved through the streets on the twenty-four mile journey to the Oudong shrine. Small groups of Buddhist monks walked prayerfully alongside the raft while the children joyfully decorated the way with colorful garlands of fresh flowers.

Directly behind the float, Alex and Sam proudly followed in the king and his royal party's vehicle.

"I guess this makes us famous," Sam whispered jokingly next to Alex's ear. "You need to work on your wave though."

Alex elbowed him playfully and mimicked the Queen of England's royal wave.

"Don't get too used to this, Sam. Our next adventure might not be as glamorous."

The ALEX HUNT Adventures continue in The ALPHA STRAIN. Available in eBook and Paperback (https://books2read.com/GetAlphaStrain)

The last hominin fossil is missing and a powerful enemy won't stop until he gets it.

Recruited by the United Nations, Alex and Sam set off on their most dangerous mission yet. Tasked to find and retrieve the last remaining fossil evidence from a death-defying underground cave system, they soon come face-to-face with a nation in conflict against each other. Caught in the crossfire of a country plunged into a historically charged political war, keeping their wits about them and allegiance to their mission are the only things keeping them from being killed.

Origins mystery meets riveting archaeological adventure thriller in the third page-turning book in the Alex Hunt Adventure Thriller series.

Inspired by true historical facts and events. Also suitable as a standalone novel.

*Includes Bonus content and a free digital copy of the series prequel.

Receive a FREE copy of the prequel and see where it all started!

NOT AVAILABLE ANYWHERE ELSE!

Click on image or enter http://download.urcelia.com in your browser

MORE BOOKS BY URCELIA TEIXEIRA

<u>ALEX HUNT Adventure Thrillers</u>

Also suited as standalone novels

The PAPUA INCIDENT - Prequel (sign up to get it FREE)

The RHAPTA KEY

The GILDED TREASON

The ALPHA STRAIN

The DAUPHIN DECEPTION

The BARI BONES

The CAIAPHAS CODE

FREE BONUS - FOR YOUR EYES ONLY!

She's a highly skilled antiquities recoverer with the unrivaled ability to eradicate criminals in the archaeology world.

Receive an exclusive free copy of her classified files.

Available for your eyes only! (http://bit.ly/Meet-Alex-Hunt)

(Not available anywhere else!)

If you enjoyed this book, I would sincerely appreciate it if you could take the time to **leave a review**. It would mean so much to me!
For sneak previews, free books and more,
Join my mailing list

BEHIND THE BOOK - AUTHOR NOTES

BASED ON TRUE EVENTS

In December 2013, a guard outside a mountain shrine in Phnom Penh, Cambodia was woken by a barking dog and found the lock to the shrine's door broken and their sacred golden urn, missing.

They said that the urn contained the hair, teeth, and bones of Buddha's body and had been respected by Buddhist followers for thousands of years.

Relics such as this one, have enormous religious and cultural significance for Cambodians. The golden urn is believed to have been brought from Sri Lanka to Cambodia in the 1950's to celebrate 2,500 years since Buddha's birth. In 2002, Norodom Sihanouk who was the king at the time, moved the relic forty-five kilometers away, from the capital city Phnom Penh to Oudong. Tens of thousands of religious followers attended the ceremony in honor of their king and Buddha.

But the unexpected theft of this sacred relic sparked a nation-wide manhunt and prompted an outcry amongst Buddhists across Cambodia. There were those followers who doubted it was the original holy urn, to begin with, and insisted on proof of its authenticity.

Police officials interrogated thirteen of the guards and subsequently detained six of them.

A mere two months after its disappearance, authorities found the missing golden urn during a house raid in Oudong, about 130 kilometers from the shrine where it got stolen.

However, to this day, none of the detainees delivered the mastermind or motives behind the theft of the golden urn.

The urn's authenticity is still in doubt and has never been proven.

For more on the golden urn and its significance, please visit www.urcelia.com/blog

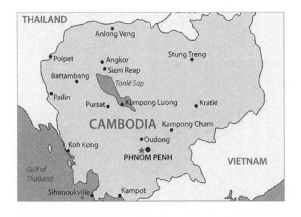

No-Spam Newsletter
ELITE SQUAD

FOLLOW Urcelia Teixeira

BookBub has a New Release Alert. Not only can you check out the latest deals, but you can also get an email when I release my next book by following me here

https://www.bookbub.com/authors/urcelia-teixeira

Website:
https://www.urcelia.com

Facebook:
https://www.facebook.com/urceliabooks

Twitter:
https//www.twitter.com/UrceliaTeixeira

ABOUT THE AUTHOR

Urcelia Teixeira is an author of fast-paced archaeological action-adventure novels with a Christian nuance.

Her Alex Hunt Adventure Thriller Series has been described by readers as 'Indiana Jones meets Lara Croft with a twist of Bourne'. She read her first book when she was four and wrote her first poem when she was seven. And though she lived vicariously through books, and her far too few travels, life happened. She married the man of her dreams and birthed three boys (and added two dogs, a cat, three chickens, and some goldfish!) So, life became all about settling down and providing a means to an end. She climbed the corporate ladder, exercised her entrepreneurial flair and made her mark in real estate.

Traveling and exploring the world made space for child-friendly annual family holidays by the sea. The ones where she succumbed to building sandcastles and barely got past reading the first five pages of a book. And on the odd occasion she managed to read fast enough to page eight, she was confronted with a moral dilemma as the umpteenth expletive forced its way off just about every page!

But by divine intervention, upon her return from yet another male-dominated camping trip, when fifty knocked hard and fast on her door, and she could no longer stomach the profanities in her reading material, she drew a line in the sand and bravely set off to create a new adventure!

It was in the dark, quiet whispers of the night, well past midnight late in the year 2017, that Alex Hunt was born.

Her philosophy

From her pen flow action-packed adventures for the armchair traveler who enjoys a thrilling escape. Devoid of the usual profanity and obscenities, she incorporates real-life historical relics and mysteries from exciting places all over the world. She aims to kidnap her reader from the mundane and plunge them into feel-good riddle-solving quests filled with danger, sabotage, and mystery!

For more visit www.urcelia.com or email her on books@urcelia.com

facebook.com/urceliateixeira

twitter.com/urcelia_teixeira

instagram.com/urceliateixeira

Paperback © ISBN: 978-0-6399665-1-9

Independently Published by Urcelia Teixeira

www.urcelia.com

books@urcelia.com

ACKNOWLEDGMENTS

- Buddhist Excerpts taken from "Eight Verses for Developing the Good Heart," written 1,000 years ago by Dorje Senge of Langri Tang

- Facts compiled from Fox News, Daily Mail, Phnom Penh Post & NY Daily News